B
and the
Dragators

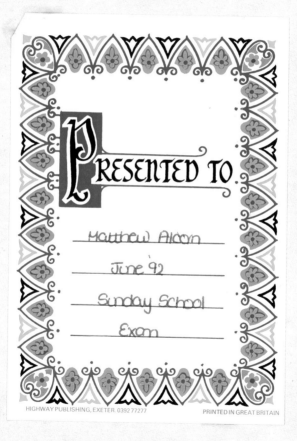

PRESENTED TO

Matthew Aldom

June '92

Sunday School

Exam

HIGHWAY PUBLISHING, EXETER. 0392 77277

Other books in this series:
The Adventures of Captain Al Scabbard
The Mystery Prowler
Skunk For Rent
The Hopeless Hen
The Dumb Dog
Duncan the Rat

Brill

and the

Dragators

Peggy Downing

Illustrated by
Anne Feiza

Scripture Press

Amersham-on-the-Hill, Bucks HP6 6JQ, England

© 1987 by Peggy Downing
First published in the USA by Victor Books a division
of Scripture Press Publications Inc. Wheaton, Illinois, USA.

First British edition 1989

ISBN 0 946515 68 9

Production and printing in Great Britain for
SCRIPTURE PRESS FOUNDATION (UK) LTD
Raans Road, Amersham-on-the-Hill, Bucks HP6 6JQ by
Nuprint Ltd, 30b Station Road, Harpenden, Herts AL5 4SE.

Contents

1	The Test	9
2	From Farm to Palace	19
3	Palace Dangers	26
4	Trapped!	36
5	News of Brill's Father	45
6	Segra's Dangerous Plan	54
7	Disaster!	66
8	New Prisoner	77
9	Prison Visit	87
10	The Dungeon	96
11	Dark Tunnel	108
12	Underwater Surprise	118
	Life in Exitorn	126

for my mother,
Hannah Hayland

Palatial Island

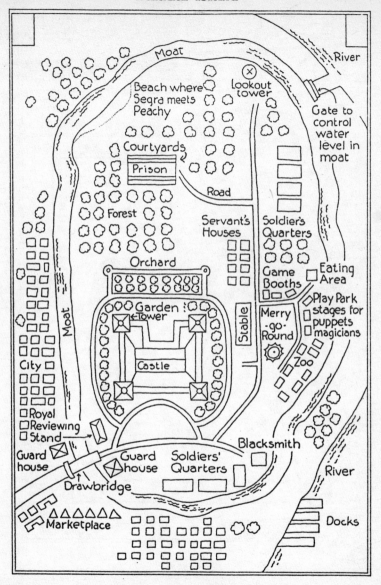

Moat

River

Beach where Seqra meets Peachy

Lookout tower

Gate to control water level in moat

Courtyards

Prison

Road

Servant's Houses

Soldier's Quarters

Forest

Orchard

Game Booths

Eating Area

Garden

Tower

Merry -go- Round

Play Park stages for puppets magicians

Stable

Zoo

Castle

City

Royal Reviewing Stand

Blacksmith

Guard house

Guard house

Soldiers' Quarters

River

Drawbridge

Marketplace

Docks

1

The Test

*T*HE MORNING SUN began to burn off the misty clouds from the jagged mountains surrounding the little town of Grebing. Brill, who had been looking for a lost lamb since dawn, stopped as he heard a faint bleating.

'Curly, is that you?' he shouted. Brill ran towards the sound and pulled the bleating lamb from the prickly bush. Cuddling the trembling animal close to him, he hurried home.

As he opened the gate to the field, his mother called, 'Brill, you'll be late for school!'

'I found Curly!' he called.

He ran to the doorway of the small stone cottage and handed the lamb to his mother. 'Can you pull the prickles from her wool? I have to hurry.'

'Don't go through the woods,' she warned.

'Mum, I have to take the shortcut or I'll be late.'

'Brill, people have seen dragators* in the woods.'

---

* You can find an explanation of the starred words under 'Life in Exitorn' on pages 126—127.

'I'll be careful.' He darted towards the forest path, but his heart pounded in his ears. He hated the spooky woods, but he dreaded Teacher Lorgett's scolding more.

Brill swallowed hard and began running through the forest. Soon he had to stop running to push the ferns and creepers apart so that he could squeeze through. He wished he had a sword to chop his way. Thorns scratched his bare legs and caught on his homespun brown tunic.

A canopy of green leaves shut out the sunlight. Brill shivered in the damp cold. The wind whined through the trees—or was that a dragator howling? *If only I had a sword,* he thought.

Brill imagined a dragator appearing in the path ahead of him. He had never seen one, but he had heard stories. Dragators were half-alligator and half-dragon. They liked to lie partly underwater in the rivers, but they could chase their prey across land. They killed fast with their fiery breath, their poisonous fangs, and their knife-like teeth.

He waved his imaginary sword in the air. If a dragator dared to breathe on him, he'd chop off its head.

'Ahhh!' Brill shrieked. He had run into a spider's web which clung to his face. He could feel invisible spiders running around on his bare skin. He brushed his face and curly brown hair with his hands. What if a big, black spider had slipped under his tunic to bite him?

Brill sighed. Why was he imagining killing dragators when he was even afraid of spiders?

The path was clearer now and Brill again ran. Just as he came to the end of the woods, he could hear the school bell ringing. His breath came in ragged gasps, and his side ached.

Two brown horses stood in front of a soldier's grey cart in the school yard. What were soldiers doing at school today? A hard knot formed in Brill's stomach. He was afraid of soldiers. They took people from their villages to serve the Exalted Emperor—innocent people who were seldom heard of again. That's what had happened to his father.

Should I go back home? I could pretend to be sick, Brill told himself. But he shuddered at the thought of what would happen if someone found him hiding from the emperor's soldiers.

He took a deep breath and hurried towards the wooden schoolhouse.

As he entered his room, Teacher Lorgett looked up. 'You're late.'

'I'm sorry, Ma'am. One of our lambs was in trouble.' Brill cringed as he saw a stocky soldier glaring at him from the back of the room. The man wore bright yellow which meant he was stationed on Palatial Island. Warriors wore olive green.

The soldier snapped, 'The emperor expects promptness from *all* his subjects!'

The teacher surprised Brill by defending him. 'Brill has an excellent record. I do not allow my pupils to be tardy without a good excuse, Soldier Algo.'

The soldier turned to Brill. 'How old are you?'

'Twelve, sir.'

'Come with me.'

Brill's heart hammered so loud he wondered if the grim-faced soldier could hear it. Algo led Brill to a room where all the boys his age were receiving instructions from a tall, muscular soldier.

Algo interrupted him to say, 'Newfel, here's a latecomer.'

Newfel glared at Brill. 'Sit down,' he ordered.

Brill slipped into a seat by the wooden table. He took great gulps of air, hoping to slow down his pounding heart.

Newfel passed out paper, saying, 'Do your best, boys.'

Brill realized it was a test but he didn't have any idea what it was for. In two years' time when he was fourteen, he'd take the career examination. Boys with high scores were appointed to government jobs. Those who scored low were left to farm the land. Brill had made up his mind to score low. His father was gone, his grandfather was old, and his mother couldn't run the farm by herself.

Newfel read the questions while the boys scratched their answers with goose quill pens.* Horn inkwells* stood in holes in the table. Brill wanted no part of government service, so he decided to write down the wrong answers.

'What is a rectangle?' asked the soldier.

Brill wrote: *It's a mess where things are wrecked and tangled up*.

'Question two. What pumps blood in to your body?'

Your stomak. Brill decided if he spelled right, they might suspect he was faking his stupidity.

'What is the greatest book in the empire?'

The Life of Immane, the Exalted Emperor of Exitorn. Brill decided he should give the expected answer here. He didn't want anyone to think he was a rebel.

Newfel droned on. 'What kind of trees grow from acorns?'

Shoe trees. Brill grinned.

'Add 7, 9, and 3.'

Brill wrote: *793*.

'What is the difference between a spider and an ant?'

Spiders eat bugs and ants bug eaters. Brill put his hand over his mouth to muffle a laugh. He continued writing nonsensical answers until Newfel had read the last question.

The soldier collected the papers and said, 'Boys, I'm going to tell you a secret. The student who does best in this examination will go to the palace to be a companion to the crown prince.'

A murmur of excitement rose from the other boys.

Newfel continued, 'We are giving this test to every twelve-year-old boy in the empire. The emperor does not want the search limited to only the high born. He believes all should have an equal chance at honours.'

That sounded good, but everyone knew the emperor had killed all those of noble birth when he took over the country.

Newfel said, 'You may go back to your room now. Good luck.'

Pront, Brill's best friend, whispered as they walked down the corridor, 'I hope I get picked.'

'I'd rather stay on the farm,' said Brill.

'Don't you want to live in the palace?'

Brill shook his head.

'You're strange, Brill.'

When the boys returned to their room, Teacher Lorgett asked the class, 'How many of you can tell me how Immane became emperor?'

Every hand shot up. It was dangerous not to know the answer.

She called on Brill. He stood and said, 'Emperor Immane was a poor man who wanted to help his people, so he gathered an army to overthrow nasty King Talder. The emperor made life better for everyone in Exitorn.' Brill sat down. He had recited what was expected, even though he knew most of the people were much poorer now than when King Talder ruled. The only people who received good salaries were the gatherers who collected the crops, the army leaders, and the secret spies whose presence scared people so they didn't dare talk against the government.

School was dismissed at eleven so the children could go home to help with the work. As they walked, they chattered about the test.

Pront bragged, 'I think I answered all the questions right. I'm going to go home and pack.'

Grinseth wrinkled her nose. 'If you're going to the palace, you won't wear homespuns. You'll get silky-smooth clothes. I think it's unfair that only boys take the test.'

Pront laughed loudly. 'The prince wouldn't want a *girl* for his companion.'

Brill said, 'I don't know why you want to go to Palatial Island. If you make the emperor angry, he throws you in the moat, and the dragators eat you.'

'Oh Brill—he wouldn't do that to a boy,' said Grinseth.

Pront added, 'Only rebels get eaten by the dragators. Are you a rebel?'

Brill felt a shiver of fear. 'Of course not. My father is serving the emperor.'

Brill hoped his friends didn't detect the bitterness he felt towards the emperor for taking away his father when Brill was only eight. Brill's mother had received only one message from her husband. Soon after he left, he wrote that he had been assigned as a palace groundskeeper.

One by one Brill's friends left to go to their houses until Brill was alone. He hurried to the small stone cottage he shared with his mother and grandfather.

He stepped inside where he could smell bread baking in the big stone fireplace.

'How was school today, Brill?' asked Mother.

Brill told her about the test. 'But don't worry, Mother. I put down wrong answers so no one will think I'm smart enough to work at the palace.' He put his arm around her waist. 'I don't want to leave you.'

Grandfather sat in a wooden chair near the fire combing his grey beard. 'King Talder built the schools to help boys and girls, but Emperor Immane has turned them into places where children are told over and over again how great Immane is.'

Brill nodded. 'It gets boring to keep talking and reading about the emperor.'

'When King Talder ruled our land, we knew he loved us and wanted us to be happy. Emperor Immane only cares about his own comfort and pleasure.'

'You mustn't *say* things like that,' cried mother. 'The emperor's spies are everywhere!'

'I'm an old man. I'm ready to meet my God. I'm not afraid of that selfish oaf sitting on the throne.'

'Father, I need you. Please, don't get yourself arrested.'

'The Holy Book says, "Good will triumph over evil."'

Mother pleaded, 'You know it's forbidden to talk about the Holy Book.'

'I know. The emperor made us burn them. He was afraid people would read the Holy Book and realize how evil he is. When I see children growing up without God's laws to guide them, rage burns inside me.'

Mother patted his shoulder. 'There's nothing you can do to change things, Father. You're only one man.'

'But I could tell people what the Holy Book said. I memorized many parts.'

Brill was alarmed. 'Grandfather, if you go around quoting the Holy Book, you'll be arrested.'

'Ah, yes, I'll be arrested. But the emperor only controls my mortal life. My soul belongs to God.'

Mother took the bread from the fireplace. Brill could hardly wait for it to cool enough to slice.

After he ate, Brill went out to do his jobs. He picked apples and plums from the orchard, and gathered carrots, corn, and cabbage from the garden. At the end of the week, the emperor's gatherers would come to pick up the fresh produce.* Near the palace was a large city where people made fine clothes and beautiful furniture for the royal family. These workers had to be fed from the farms. The peasants were only allowed to keep enough food and wool for their own needs.

When Brill crawled into bed that night, he couldn't sleep. Grandfather said God still loved the people of Exitorn, even though Immane had proclaimed that he was to be worshipped. 'Please God, take care of my father; help him find some way to send a message to us. Watch over Mother. She works so hard. And don't let Grandfather be arrested.'

* * * * *

On Monday morning Brill walked with his friends to school.

Pront said, 'I hope we'll hear who is going to the palace.'

Brill pointed out, 'There are hundreds of villages and cities throughout the empire, so there isn't much chance they'll pick someone from our little school.'

Pront shrugged. 'You may be right. But when I'm fourteen, I'll do my best on the final test so I'll get a good assignment. Maybe I can be a palace guard.'

'Won't you be sorry to leave your family?' Brill asked.

'Yes, but I'm never going to get rich on a farm.'

Grinseth laughed. 'You'll never get rich working for the emperor either. He keeps most of the wealth for himself.'

Pront cried, 'Grinseth, are you a rebel?'

'Of course not.' Grinseth's eyes reflected fear. 'I—I just meant that the emperor was the only one wise enough to handle the wealth of our country.'

Brill thought how uncomfortable it was to have to be so careful of everything you said.

As they came near the schoolhouse, they saw the grey cart parked in front.

'Oh, oh, what do the soldier's want now?' asked Brill.

'Perhaps one of us has been picked for the prince's companion,' Pront said, then he broke into a run.

Brill trudged on. He took deep breaths trying to get rid of the queasy feeling that something terrible was about to happen.

Grinseth watched him, 'What's wrong, Brill?'

'Nothing,' he snapped. He wished he knew how to control the fear that swept over him when he saw the emperor's soldiers.

The school bell rang and the children hurried to their rooms. Teacher Lorgett stood in front of Brill's class. 'Boys and girls, Soldier Newfel has an important announcement.'

'Today is a great day for the village of Grebing. Out of all the thousands of boys in the empire, a boy from your school has been chosen for a high position in our government.'

The soldier stopped a moment. The children leaned forward in their seats. The suspense was unbearable.

Newfel pulled a paper from his pocket, unfolded it, and began to read, 'By order of Immane, Exalted Emperor of Exitorn, you are summoned to report immediately to the palace to serve as companion to Prince Grossder.' He looked at the class. 'Who is the boy named Brill?'

Brill felt fireballs exploding in his head. He stood, clutching the table for support.

The soldier handed him the paper with the emperor's crest emblazoned in gold. 'The summons is addressed to you, Brill.'

'Thank you, sir.' Brill took the paper. His legs felt like jelly as he slumped to his seat.

The class clapped.

Soldier Newfel spoke. 'We'll take you home to say good-bye. Then we're off to the palace. If we hurry, we can be there tomorrow night. You're a very lucky boy.'

But Brill didn't *feel* lucky at all. *I deliberately put the wrong answers on the test,* he thought. *The whole thing must be a terrible mistake!*

2

From Farm to Palace

*B*RILL CLIMBED INTO THE CART and sat on the wooden seat between the two soldiers. The driver cracked his whip and the horses plodded forward. As the wheels rattled on the rutted dirt road, the cart lurched from side to side. Brill tried to swallow the lump in his throat.

Newfel asked, 'Ever seen the palace, Brill?'

'No, sir.'

'It's huge. I haven't ever been inside. You're lucky. I wish I could live in the palace.'

The other soldier smiled. 'Palatial Island is the most beautiful place in Exitorn.'

Brill pointed. 'There's my house.'

Newfel said, 'No need to take anything. You'll get whatever you need at the palace.'

'Probably silk clothes and gold combs,' added Algo.

Brill jumped to the ground. His heart pounded as he ran to the door and threw it open.

His mother stopped sweeping. 'Why are you home so early?'

Brill threw his arms around his mother's frail frame.

'What's wrong?' she asked.

He tried to swallow his tears so that he could talk. 'Palace. I have to go to the palace,' he gasped.

'When?'

'Right now. Oh Mother, I don't want to go.'

Grandfather stirred the fire with a poker. 'That's an evil place. He who lives only for pleasure starves his soul.'

Brill saw the tears glistening in his mother's eyes, but she spoke calmly. 'What are you to do at the palace?'

'I'll be Prince Grossder's companion.'

'You must do the best job you can. Perhaps you'll see your father. Try to send word to me. I know it's hard to get anyone to carry a message. No one wants to be accused of spying.'

'If I can, I'll send a letter.'

'I'll pray for you every day,' said his Mother.

'How will you do all the work on the farm?'

'Grandfather and I will manage.'

'Who will find Curly when she gets lost?'

'We'll take good care of Curly. Don't worry.'

They heard loud knocking. Grandfather hobbled to the door, while Brill hugged his mother again.

'Our love will travel over the miles,' she whispered, kissing his forehead.

Brill broke away as the door opened.

Newfel spoke in a gruff voice. 'Time to go.'

Brill swallowed his tears, said good-bye to his mother and grandfather, and rejoined the men on the cart.

He tried not to think of how long it might be before he'd see his mother again. He didn't want the soldiers to know how much he hurt inside.

'Don't look so sad,' Newfel said. 'Most boys would give anything to live like a prince.'

'I worry about how Mother will do all the work on the farm. Grandfather can't get around very well.'

Newfel lowered his voice. 'Don't talk about your mother at the palace. The emperor wants his servants to concentrate on their new jobs. You've received a great honour. Forget about your past.'

'I'll try, sir,' answered Brill, but he'd never forget his mother. As they bounced along the rough roads through villages and patches of woods and over bridges and hills, Brill let his mind imagine how things might be.

He'd find his father, and together they'd escape from Palatial Island. They'd buy a cart and horses and hurry back to Mother and Grandfather. They'd all go to a far country where they could be together.

It was a comforting dream though his practical side pointed out the difficulties. Even if he found his father, how would they get off Palatial Island? It was surrounded by a wide moat filled with water and fierce dragators. Brill told himself, *If I find Father, he'll find a way for us to go back to Mother. But if there is a way, why hasn't he come back sooner?*

They stopped at a small inn for lunch. The men ate heartily, dipping hard rolls into the beef and vegetable stew and chewing noisily.

Algo nudged Newfel. 'We aren't setting a very good example for Brill here. We should be using our best palace manners.'

Newfel laughed. 'From what I hear, Emperor Immane eats like a starved pig.'

Algo cried, 'Newfel, take care! When Brill gets to the palace, he'll tell the prince what you said—and the next thing you know, you'll be chewed up by hungry dragators.'

Newfel rubbed his hands together nervously. 'Ah, Brill, I was only joking. I didn't mean to sound disrespectful.

Please, forget what I said.' Newfel pulled a gold coin from his pocket and pushed it towards Brill. 'We're friends. Here's a little something to seal our friendship.'

'You don't have to pay me.' Brill pushed the coin back to him. 'I won't say anything to get you in trouble.'

Brill forced himself to eat a little food, hoping it might fill the empty hole in his stomach, but the hollow remained. It was from fear, not hunger. The food sat in his stomach, a hard uncomfortable lump.

They climbed back into the cart, and Brill felt his lump of lunch bounce around. He felt sick, but he fought the queasy feeling, ordering his stomach to calm down.

'You look a little green,' said Newfel.

'I'm all right.'

'Better sit by the edge. Then you can hang your head out, if anything comes up.'

Brill changed places with him. He wished he could escape the lurching cart.

That evening they slept on the floor in the main room of a roadside inn. Newfel asked for a blanket for each of them. Brill didn't sleep. The stone floor was hard, a stranger mumbled in his sleep, and cold draughts blew under the door. Brill's tears fell on the old, stained blanket. He longed for home.

* * * * *

The next afternoon they reached Palatial Island.

'There's the palace.' Algo pointed to the stone towers rising against the blue sky.

The narrow street widened into a boulevard between green lawns and trees. The boulevard led to the draw-bridge. The huge castle was surrounded by shrubs, trees, and flower gardens. Brill wondered if his father worked there. Finding his father was his one ray of hope.

The soldiers stopped their cart by a guardhouse where they handed their permit to the head guard. They were waved on.

A line of twelve soldiers with swords stood on either side of the road.

As they crossed the drawbridge, Brill looked down and shivered. A dragator lifted his long scaly neck and opened his huge mouth showing long, pointed teeth and a smoking breath. Another dragator lay floating near the shore, and Brill guessed he was over fifteen feet long.

Algo whispered, 'They say a dragator's breath can cook a man in an instant.'

'Makes it handy for the dragator. He can roast his meal before he chews it,' added Newfel.

Algo said, 'Watch your step, Brill. If the emperor gets angry with you, he'll toss you to the dragators.'

'Ah, don't scare the boy like that,' said Newfel.

'It's better for him to know what dangers he's facing so that he can be alert,' argued Algo.

Brill's queasy stomach gurgled, protesting the fear signals from his brain.

Newfel went on talking as if to make Brill forget his fears. 'The water in the moat comes from the river. Gates control the amount of water and keep the dragators from escaping.'

The cart climbed the hill towards the palace and stopped in the circular driveway. Newfel advised Brill, 'Show your summons to the doorkeeper. He'll show you where to go.'

'Thanks for the ride.' Brill pulled the summons from his pocket, and jumped off the cart.

The dour-faced doorkeeper stared at him. 'What does the likes of you want here?'

Brill handed him the summons. He had a sudden wild hope the man would send him home. It would be a long walk, but he'd find his way.

The man's manner changed abruptly. 'Master Brill, the prince has been waiting for you.'

He called for another servant. 'Take Master Brill to the prince's wing.'

'Yes, sir,' the servant answered. He turned to Brill. 'Follow me.'

Brill's eyes grew wide with wonder as he stared at the gold columns, crystal chandeliers, and elaborate scenes painted on the walls. He followed his guide up a white stone staircase and down a carpeted corridor. The servant knocked on a carved door. A tall, thin man with a stern face answered.

'This is Brill,' explained the servant, handing the man the summons.

The man frowned as he looked at Brill's shabby clothes. 'Follow me. My name is Meopar. I'm chief steward for the prince. If you have questions about proper procedure, it's best to ask me. Don't bother the prince with questions and don't depend on servants of lesser ranks to know the right answer.'

Brill nodded.

Meopar opened a door. 'Prince Grossder, your new companion has arrived.'

The prince sat on a huge upholstered chair. It needed to be large to hold the prince's weight. Brill had never seen anyone as fat.

'Come closer,' Prince Grossder commanded.

Brill approached his chair.

'What's the difference between ants and spiders?'

'Well, spiders spin webs and . . .'

'No, no—I want the answer you put on your test.'

'Oh, you mean the one about spiders eat bugs and ants bug eaters.'

The prince chuckled. 'I really liked that one. When we go on picnics in the forest, we bring soldiers to keep the ants away from our food.'

Brill had the sinking feeling his clever scheme to look stupid had led him to the palace.

Prince Grossder continued, 'I told the fellow who was correcting the tests to show me the ones that had originality. I didn't want some brain who knows everything as my companion. He'd be a deadly bore. I picked you, Brill, because you can make me laugh.'

Brill gulped. He had never thought of himself as a comedian.

3

Palace Dangers

*H*AVE YOU had dinner yet?' the prince asked.

Brill shook his head. 'I'm not very hungry. That cart ride took away my appetite. My stomach felt like an egg being whipped by a beater.'

The prince laughed. 'I'm very hungry.' He called, 'Meopar, tell the maids to bring my dinner. Bring some for Brill too.'

Prince Grossder pointed to a small upholstered chair. 'Sit down, Brill. Where did you get those ugly clothes?'

'My mother made them for me out of the wool from our sheep.'

'They look scratchy. I'll have my tailor measure you for new clothes first thing in the morning.'

'Thank you, sir.' Brill struggled to be polite, though he didn't want to replace the clothes his mother had made. He blinked away a tear as he thought of her spinning the thread, weaving the cloth, and then sewing the garments.

A maid in white entered with a large tray of food and placed it on the table by the prince. A second maid came with a smaller tray and placed it on the table by Brill.

He studied the food. He didn't recognize anything. Items were of different shapes and sizes, but everything was brown. One of the maids poured him a glass of brown liquid.

Brill watched the prince pick up a piece of brown stuff with his gold fork and bite into it.

Brill lifted his fork. His stomach fluttered as his eyes relayed the message it was about to receive something strange. Brill didn't know whether to eat or not. He didn't want to upset his uneasy stomach.

As he heard the prince choking, he looked up in alarm. Meopar, who always stayed close, ran to the prince.

Prince Grossder waved him away. 'Something went down the wrong way. I couldn't help laughing. Brill, you are so funny! The expression on your face when the maid brought your food.'

Brill explained, 'I've never seen food like this before. What is it, sir?'

The prince laughed even louder.

Brill's face grew hot, but he forced a smile as if he too were enjoying the joke.

Finally the prince stopped laughing long enough to say, 'Tonight we're having steak cubes, carrot slices, roast potatoes, and cherry tomatoes. It's all stuff I hate, but Mother says it's good for me.'

Brill didn't see any of those things on his plate, but he speared a cube with his fork and put it in his mouth. It was sweet and soft, like nothing he had tasted before. But as he chewed he found a piece of meat inside the strange brown stuff. The next piece was a carrot. The brown coating gave everything a strange taste. Even the liquid in his glass had the same sweet taste.

Prince Grossder's round face broke into a wide smile. 'I hope you like chocolate.'

'Is that the brown stuff?' asked Brill.

'Haven't you ever had chocolate?'

Brill shook his head. 'No, sir.'

'I don't suppose peasants have any way to get it. My father sends his ships to a faraway land to get cacao beans.* I'd like to just eat chocolate, but Mother says I must eat other things too. It was her idea to have all my food dipped in chocolate. That's the only way I'll eat most things. Have you finished?'

'I've eaten all I can.'

The prince shrugged. 'You need to eat more then you won't be so scrawny.'

Brill wanted to point out that he wasn't scrawny unless he was being compared to someone as fat as a hippopotamus. But he didn't say anything.

The prince called Meopar. 'Ring the maids to bring dessert.' He looked at Brill. 'This is the best part.'

The maids hurried and removed their trays. Another woman came in with a large dessert tray and two plates. Brill looked at a brown layer cake, a cream pie, and a bowl of sweets—all chocolate.

Under the prince's direction, the maid cut him a large piece of cake and a huge piece of pie.

The maid turned to Brill. 'What would you like, sir?'

'A small piece of cake, please,' answered Brill.

The prince reached his podgy hands into the bowl. 'Here, have some sweets. You'll find nuts, cherries, caramels—all sorts of delicious things inside the chocolate.'

'Thank you very much,' Brill said, but he'd have swopped all this sweet food for one slice of his mother's bread.

Finally the prince waved away the dessert tray. He stood up with some effort and waddled to the door. 'I'll show you your room, Brill.'

Prince Grossder walked through his own large bedroom where a huge gold bed stood in the centre. He opened a door. 'Here's your room.'

Brill gasped. 'It's beautiful.' The wooden bed and chest of drawers were decorated with mother-of-pearl.* A fur rug covered most of the floor.

Prince Grossder opened the wardrobe. 'My last companion was plumper than you, but you can probably wear his clothes until the tailor makes yours.'

Brill felt the soft, silky fabric of the brightly coloured tunics.

'You'll find a night shirt in a drawer,' said the prince.

'Tell Meopar to throw out your old clothes. They're not suitable for the palace.'

Brill nodded. 'Yes, your highness.'

'Better go to bed. Tomorrow will be busy,' said the prince. 'You'll meet the emperor and the queen and my sister Florette. Everyone likes her, but I don't like her companion. The best part of tomorrow will be showing you my play park. The maids bring me my breakfast in bed. I'll tell them to wake you so you can eat with me.'

The prince left and Brill pulled a silky robe from a drawer. He liked the smooth feel of the cloth next to his skin. He looked around for somewhere to hide his home-spuns. He couldn't throw out the clothes his mother had made. He finally stuffed them in the bottom drawer of a chest of drawers under an extra blanket. He hoped no one would find them there.

Then Brill crawled into the soft bed. He felt as if he were lying on a cloud, one of the fluffy white ones that looked like cotton. How fast his life had changed. He ached to be home again with his mother and grandfather.

He tried to guess why the prince's former companion left all his fancy clothes. Maybe he had outgrown them or the prince was so stingy, he wouldn't let him take them, or perhaps.... But he fell asleep before he finished the thought.

Brill awoke early the next morning. Everything was quiet. He missed the sounds of home: the cockerel crowing, Mother building a fire, Grandfather still snoring. Brill walked to the window and peeked out between the green velvet curtains. A thick forest of tall evergreens surrounded a clearing. In the middle stood a stone building enclosed by a wall. He wondered what it was. To the left was the moat. He shuddered as he thought of the man-eating dragators.

Brill picked an orange tunic from the wardrobe. The shoulders hung halfway to his elbows, and he tied a cord around his waist to make it fit a little better. He pulled on a pair of white hose. The shoes with curly, pointed toes were much too big, so Brill slipped on his old leather sandals.

What would the children at school say if they could see his fine clothes? He grinned as he imagined walking through the town surprising everyone.

He opened the door to the landing and stepped out. No one seemed to be stirring. Apparently, people in palaces slept longer than people on farms. Brill longed for some fresh air. He crept to the end of the landing where he found a stairway. He tiptoed down. At the bottom he saw halls leading in different directions, and he had an uneasy feeling if he went much farther he wouldn't be able to find his way back.

'Are you lost?'

Brill jumped and turned to see a blonde girl a head shorter than he. She had a turned-up nose and saucy blue eyes.

'I'm not lost,' he answered.

'Are you the prince's new companion?'

He nodded. 'I'm Brill. Who are you?'

'Segra, Princess Florette's companion. Want to see the garden?'

'Yes,' he answered. 'When do people get up around here?'

'The members of the royal family usually sleep until noon. But I don't mind. I like having some time to myself. If you think being agreeable, cheerful, and amusing all the time is easy, you'll soon find out differently.'

'I never wanted to come here,' Brill whispered.

'Don't let anyone else hear you say that,' warned Segra. She led the way down the halls, making several turns until she came to a door. She pushed it open and they stepped out into the gardens.

Brill breathed deeply of the sweet-scented air. 'The fresh air makes me hungry.'

'Let's walk to the orchard. The peaches are ripe.'

The orchard was at the end of the formal gardens. Brill picked a peach and bit into its juicy sweetness. Segra ate one too. Brill didn't have a handkerchief, so he wiped his sticky hands on some leaves. 'It certainly tastes good to eat something not covered with chocolate.'

'Don't let the prince hear you say that.'

'Can't I have any opinions of my own? Do I have to agree with *everything* the prince says?'

'You'll live longer if you do.'

'What do you mean by that? And what happened to the boy who was here before me?'

'They fed him to the dragators.'

'But why? Why would they kill a boy?'

'They said he had rebel thoughts.'

An icy shiver ran up Brill's spine. Now he knew why the other boy's clothes were left hanging in the wardrobe.

'We have dangerous jobs—but if we help each other, we may survive.' Segra led the way into the forest.

'I don't see how. I've got lots of rebellious thoughts. I'm bound to say the wrong thing.'

'I didn't mean to make you nervous, but I thought you should know about the danger.' Segra sat on a fallen log. Brill sat beside her.

'The royal family are scared of the people, and the people are scared of them,' continued Segra. 'The emperor is trying to make himself secure with more and more soldiers, but that only makes the people more resentful and dangerous. If he treated everyone more kindly, he wouldn't have so much to fear.'

Brill said, 'Can't someone make him see that?'

'No, because the emperor won't listen to advice. He has a council, but they only suggest things they know the emperor will like. Nobody will risk making him angry.'

'I wish they had never picked me to move to the palace. I wonder if I'll ever see Mother and Grandfather again.' Brill's voice trembled as he thought of home.

Segra whispered, 'I've been here for two years, but I still get homesick. We didn't have soft beds or much food at home or any of the palace comforts, but I'd go back in a minute if I could.'

'What village did you come from?'

'It wasn't exactly a village. It was a settlement high on one of the Border Mountains. When the emperor took over the kingdom and took away the people's freedom, some of the people from our village escaped to the mountains.'

'What did you eat?'

'Goat's milk and cheese. We ground the seeds of the wild grasses and made flour for bread. We grew root crops. It was a hard life, but the soldiers and gatherers didn't bother us.'

Brill said, 'We lived on a farm, and we had to give most of the stuff we grew to the gatherers. It wasn't fair.'

Segra stood and stretched. 'We had better get back to the palace before we're missed.'

Brill stood too. 'If you lived way up in the mountains, how did they pick you to be Princess Florette's companion?'

'Father sent me to school in the village in the winter. All the girls took a test, and the next thing I knew I was summoned to the palace. I didn't even get time to say good-bye to my mother and father.'

'That's terrible.'

'Father says God has a plan for our lives, so maybe I've been put here for a reason. The emperor may say God doesn't exist, but that doesn't make it true. I know He does.' She glanced nervously around. 'We'd better hurry.

Oh—when we're introduced later today, pretend you haven't seen me before. We don't want to be accused of plotting against the emperor.'

'I'm too scared to do any plotting.'

'But our only hope is in helping the rebels.' Segra's whisper was so low, Brill had to bend his head close to hear.

He felt his blood grow cold. 'Do you know some rebels?'

Segra countered with another question. 'Do you want King Talder to be king again?'

Brill shivered. What if Segra had been sent to test his loyalty? 'Why are you asking?'

'I have to know how you feel. I think I can trust you, but I have to be sure.'

Brill looked at Segra's clear blue eyes. He whispered. 'I don't remember King Talder. My grandfather said things were better then.'

'I know where King Talder is.'

'Where?'

'He's in the prison in the forest. He's very weak. If we bring him extra food, maybe he'll be able to regain his strength so we can help him escape.'

'*We?*' Brill gulped. 'But if anyone gets caught helping a prisoner, he'll be fed to the dragators.'

Segra pressed her lips together, then said, 'I would do *anything* to see King Talder ruling again. My parents talked about how happy everyone was then.'

Brill and Segra walked out of the forest together and through the orchard. Brill looked around, hoping no one had heard Segra's rash words. He felt a cold sweat oozing from his pores as he remembered the dragators' sharp teeth. He made up his mind to keep away from Segra.

Nearing the palace door, she whispered, 'Will you meet me again tomorrow morning?'

'Uh, no—I don't think the prince will want me prowling around.'

'The prince will never know. He sleeps until noon.'

'I can't promise to meet you, Segra.'

'But I need your help.'

'You'll have to find somebody else.'

Brill opened the door, and Segra led the way back to his room. He went inside and closed the door. Now that he realized his life hung by a precarious* thread, Brill was determined not to do anything to upset Prince Grossder. No one would suspect him of rebellious thoughts.

4

Trapped!

AN HOUR LATER Meopar came to invite Brill to join the prince for breakfast. They ate waffles with fudge syrup and chocolate-covered sausages. Dessert was chocolate frosted doughnuts. Brill declined dessert.

While the prince was being dressed, the tailor measured Brill for new clothes.

The tailor removed a row of pins from between his lips. 'You have strong muscles. You must have worked hard.'

'I lived on a farm.'

'The prince is very flabby,' the tailor whispered. 'Perhaps you can get him to exercise. It's not healthy to eat so much without exercising.'

Brill nodded, but he knew there was not much chance he could change the prince's habits.

The royal shoemaker entered then to measure Brill's feet. He shook his head sadly when he saw the worn sandals. 'Never again will you have to wear such shabby shoes,' he promised.

When the prince was dressed, he called for Brill. 'It's a beautiful day to go to my play park. But first I'll introduce you to the rest of my family.'

Brill followed the prince as he waddled down the wide stairs and into the throne room where the emperor and queen were sitting on large thrones upholstered with gold velvet. Brill and the prince walked across the thick patterned carpet.

Brill felt panic. He should have asked Meopar what he should do and say when he met the emperor.

Emperor Immane was heavier than the prince. His puffy face was a reddish colour, and his double chins hid his neck. Queen Lera had a pretty face, and she smiled at Brill.

The prince said, 'Father and Mother, this is my new companion, Brill.'

Brill bowed on one knee. He hoped he was doing the right thing.

The emperor stared at him with hypnotic grey eyes. Finally he said, 'Stand up, boy. Are you a loyal subject of the empire?'

'Oh yes, sir.' Brill nodded vigorously.

'If you are loyal, you have a great future.'

'Thank you, your majesty.'

Brill heard a girl's voice behind him. 'Father, can Segra and I go to the city to look in the shops?'

'You'll have to take a squadron of soldiers with you,' the emperor answered. 'I never know what the rebels might do.'

'Yes, we'll take soldiers along. We'll be safe.'

Prince Grossder said, 'Florette, this is my new companion, Brill.'

'Hello,' said Florette. She was a slim girl with dark red hair and pretty features.

Brill bowed his held.

Florette added, 'My companion's name is Segra.'

'How do you do,' said Brill.

Segra smiled. 'Hello, Brill.'

'We're going to spend the day at the play park,' announced the prince.

Brill and the prince rode to the play park in a small gold carriage pulled by a team of black horses. Meopar sat beside the driver. He went wherever the prince went. His craggy face showed little expression, but his black eyes moved around constantly, watching for danger. Brill had the eerie feeling that Meopar could tell what he was thinking. He tried to suppress any rebel thoughts that flashed into his mind when he was close to Meopar.

As they entered the play park gates, Prince Grossder called to the gatekeeper, 'We want to see a puppet show and a magician.'

The gatekeeper rushed over with a blank paper, and he and Meopar worked out the day's schedule.

The prince ordered the driver to take them on a tour of the grounds. Brill was fascinated by the variety of things to see. They began at a row of game booths and ended up at a small zoo where monkeys and bears begged for handouts. The prince squealed as he threw them peanuts from the cart.

Brill remarked, 'I don't see anyone else here. Doesn't anyone else use the park?'

'Of course not. Except for Florette and Segra. When that daft King Talder ruled, he let the city people use the park—but they were noisy and threw litter all over the place. When my father took over the empire, he closed the park. Later he had it fitted up just for me. And because you're my companion, you can use it too.'

Brill nodded, 'It's very nice.'

'Hey, it's better than nice—it's stupendous! I'm probably the only prince in the world with a play park like this.'

'You're lucky,' agreed Brill.

When the carriage stopped, Brill asked, 'What's that?' He pointed to the carved horses standing on the round platform.

'Haven't you ever seen a merry-go-round?' The prince wrinkled up his nose as if Brill's stupidity was beyond him.

Brill followed Grossder onto the platform. There was a special wide horse that Brill guessed had been made for the prince. The attendant helped him mount it. Brill climbed on a horse behind the prince's. The horses began to go around as the music played. A husky fellow stood in the middle turning a crank to turn the platform.

Brill tingled with excitement. It was such fun, but then he noticed the perspiration running down the operator's face. Their fun was making him work very hard.

'Make it go faster,' shouted the prince, and the poor man strained to follow the orders.

Brill was glad when the prince finally signalled he had had enough. They returned to the carriage and rode to the puppet theatre where they watched a funny show. Brill laughed until his sides ached. The prince offered Brill chocolate-covered peanuts and raisins. Brill ate only a few, but the prince gobbled them by the handful.

The carriage moved to the magician's booth. Brill wished he knew how to do tricks like that.

When the show was over, the prince shouted, 'Better learn some new tricks. I've seen all these.'

The magician's eyes widened with fear and he answered in a hoarse voice, 'Yes, your highness.'

The prince ordered the carriage to return to the palace.

'How did you like my play park?' he asked.

'I had a great time,' answered Brill.

'There's lots more to see. We'll be back tomorrow.'

Brill asked, 'Don't you ever go to school?'

'I used to, but it was boring. I know how to read and write—that's all I need to know. When Father dies, I'll become emperor. Then I'll make the big decisions, but I'll appoint people to handle all the details. Father has a council to see that everything runs smoothly at the palace.'

Brill frowned, but he turned away so the prince wouldn't see his scowl. How could Prince Grossder think the government existed for his pleasure? Didn't he even consider the people under him?

Oh well, thought Brill. *There's nothing I can do to change things. I might as well enjoy myself. The play park is exciting. Puppet plays and merry-go-rounds are more fun than going to school and doing jobs. I'll be careful not to say anything that will annoy Prince Grossder, but other than that I can relax and enjoy myself.*

The next morning Brill again woke up early. He dressed in a red tunic and black hose. It was fun to have so many clothes to pick from, but they made him think of what had happened to his predecessor. Fear tingled his spine as he slipped out of his room. He tiptoed down to the side door Segra had shown him yesterday, hoping he wouldn't see her again.

Hungry for a peach, he ran through the garden to the orchard. As he reached for a large golden peach, a voice barked, 'And who do you think you are?'

Brill gulped and turned to see a burly man gathering peaches in a large wicker basket.

'I'm Brill, companion to Prince Grossder. I would like a peach.' Brill tried to sound important, but inside he felt fear. If he were breaking a palace rule, he might be in trouble.

The burly man laughed. 'So *you're* the new companion. Might as well enjoy yourself as long as you can. Eat as many peaches as you want.'

'What do you mean by "enjoy yourself as long as you can"?' demanded Brill.

'Prince Grossder doesn't keep his companions very long. He gets bored with everything. When you spend all your time trying to have fun, you run out of ways to enjoy yourself and life turns stale.'

Brill felt that he had finally met someone he could trust. He glanced around, then asked in a low voice, 'Do you know a man named Stronall? I believe he works at the palace grounds.'

The man's voice sank to a whisper. 'I knew him. Why are you asking?'

'He's my father.'

'Don't tell anyone else you're his son.'

'But why?'

'Can't explain now. I have to hurry back to the kitchen with this fruit.'

He walked quickly away, and Brill called, 'Please tell me if he's here,' but the man didn't answer.

Brill picked a peach and walked out of the orchard towards the forest. He shivered with fear. What kind of trouble was his father in? He had to know. But that man had warned him not to even mention his name.

He ate his peach without really tasting its sweet goodness, for he was worrying about his father. He followed a path into the woods.

He twirled as he heard a voice behind him. 'Brill, am I glad to see you!' Segra was carrying a basket of peaches and plums.

'Where are you going?' he asked.

'To the prison to take some fruit to King Talder.'

'Will they let you see him?'

'No—but I have a plan.'

Brill grimaced. He hoped Segra's warm greeting didn't mean he was part of the plan.

She continued, 'The cells all have small courtyards. King Talder built the prison. He felt that even murderers should be able to enjoy the outside air. He never dreamed he'd spend almost ten years in one of those cells he had designed.'

'Are you going to throw the fruit over the courtyard wall?' asked Brill.

She shook her head. 'You can't throw peaches. I'm going to climb a tree by the wall and then let the basket down by a rope.'

Brill noticed she had a rope tied to the basket. 'Aren't there any guards?'

'Yes, but they only walk around the prison every half hour or so. There's plenty of time. All you need to do is help me up into the tree. The lowest branch is too high for me to reach.'

Brill stopped. The penalty for helping a prisoner was death. 'I don't want to get involved in rebel stuff. It's too dangerous. 'It won't do any good.'

'I won't let King Talder die. They've cut down his food. The emperor thinks King Talder knows where some treasure is hidden. They're trying to force him to tell.'

'Why won't he tell.'

'There *is* no treasure! He sold the palace jewels so that he could build irrigation ditches and windmills to help the people have a better life. He can't tell them how to find gems he sold long ago to other monarchs.* I think they're trying to starve him, and we're the only ones who can help.'

'How do you know all this?'

'There's a little hole in the courtyard wall, and I talk to the king through that. Now that I have you to help me, it'll be a lot easier to get the food to him.' She dropped her voice and stepped behind a large maple tree. 'We have to watch here until we see the guard go by. Then I'll have time to climb the tree and lower the fruit.'

Brill tried to think how they could get the fruit in to the king without climbing the tree and risking being seen by one of the soldiers.

'Here comes the guard,' whispered Segra. 'He looks half-asleep. We don't have to be afraid of him.'

When the guard had returned to the other side of the prison, Segra stepped into the clearing and motioned Brill to follow.

'See—there's the tree.' It was a sturdy pine with long green needles. 'You help me up so that I can grab the first branch.'

'Uh, I'll climb it,' offered Brill. 'I'm taller, and I can do it faster. Here, give me the fruit and rope.'

'But you're wearing a red shirt. Why did you pick such a bright colour?'

'I didn't know I'd be helping a prisoner. Here, give me the basket and rope.'

'Let the basket of fruit down and pull it back after King Talder take the fruit out.'

Brill tied the rope and basket around his waist so his hands were free. Reaching up, he grabbed a sturdy branch and pulled himself into the tree. He glanced around. There were no guards in sight. He climbed to a large branch overhanging the small courtyard.

He saw the smiling face of an old grey-bearded man looking up at him. The king reminded Brill of his grandfather. Brill untied the rope around his waist and let down the basket.

King Talder quickly removed the peaches and plums. 'Thank you, oh, thank you,' he whispered.

Brill pulled on the basket, but the rope caught in another branch. He leaned over to wiggle it free.

'Cr-r-rack!'

The branch broke. Brill fell in the courtyard with a painful thud. His left leg crumpled under him.

King Talder cried, 'My boy, you're in great danger!'

'I know.' Brill's brain felt as if it were exploding from all the conflicting messages. *Run! Hide! Climb! Dig! Disappear!*

The shooting pain in his left ankle made him dizzy, but he tried to think. He stared at his surroundings. The high stone wall had no handholds or toeholds. The tree above was too high to reach. There was no place to hide. Soon Brill would be discovered and executed as a rebel!

5

News of Brill's Father

*H*URRY!' *KING TALDER CRIED.* 'Come to my cell. Help me carry something for you to climb on.'

Brill scrambled up, flinching as he put his weight on his left ankle.

King Talder didn't look strong enough to carry anything. Brill saw a rough wooden bench, and he dragged it out to the courtyard. He climbed on it, but it wasn't high enough to reach either the tree or the top of the wall. He hobbled back to the cell, trying to ignore his throbbing ankle.

King Talder pulled at his heavy washstand. Brill helped him and together they managed to lift it onto the bench. It wobbled. Would his only hope for escape just tumble him back into the courtyard?

'How will you get this stuff back to your cell?' he whispered.

'I'll manage. You must get out of here.'

The king held the washstand steady for Brill. Reaching upward as far as he could, Brill grabbed a branch and prayed that it wouldn't break. He pulled himself to the top of the wall. His heart sank as he saw a guard marching towards the tree. If he looked up, he'd see him. Brill climbed into the tree, flattening himself against the rough bark of the trunk. He wished the pine tree had more branches to hide him and his bright red tunic.

Then he saw Segra running towards the guard. She gestured and pointed in the other direction. Hoping Segra could keep the guard's attention focused away from him, Brill scrambled to another branch and dropped to the outside of the wall. Pain jolted through his injured ankle. Waves of dizziness tempted him to lie still and sink into pain-free unconsciousness. But he couldn't stay there.

If he were caught, he might be the main course on the dragator's dinner menu. He tried not to think of those sharp teeth biting into his flesh.

He stood and hopped to the woods on his good leg. His heart pounded in his ears as he crawled under a bush to let his throbbing ankle rest.

What a close call! he thought. *I'm going to stay away from Segra. She only gets me into trouble. It's too dangerous to help the king no matter how much he needs it.*

Brill sighed. He felt safe in his hiding place. But what about Prince Grossder? What would the prince do if he discovered Brill wasn't there when he wanted him? He had to get back.

Brill crawled out from under the bush. He found a stout stick which helped relieve the weight from his aching ankle. He limped along the forest path.

When Brill returned to his room, he found Meopar waiting for him. 'The prince wants to see you,' he barked.

Brill walked slowly into the prince's bedroom, trying not to limp.

'You weren't here when I summoned you,' complained Prince Grossder.

46

'I'm sorry, your highness. I merely went outside to pick a peach. I hope I didn't do something wrong.'

'Not wrong—just stupid. All you have to do is pull the cord above your bed, and a servant will bring you what you want. You don't have to go out and pick peaches yourself.'

Brill nodded, then added, 'The gardens are lovely first thing in the morning. I enjoyed my short walk to the orchard.'

Prince Grossder's eyes flashed fire. 'Don't argue with me! I want you here when I need you!'

'Yes, your highness. Whatever you say.'

The maids entered with breakfast. Chocolate chip pancakes with fudge sauce, and chocolate-coated fruit— pitted prunes, peach wedges, and grapes.

As the prince gobbled his breakfast, he seemed to forget his anger at Brill.

The prince was in a good mood when he and Brill left to spend the day at the play park. They repeated some of the things they had done before and also watched a trained seal act and a demonstration of acrobats.

The top acrobat in a pyramid of six men fell. Though he walked away, Brill noticed his terrified expression. It was dangerous to make a mistake before the prince.

'He had better not fall again or I'll replace him,' muttered the prince.

One the way home, Prince Grossder asked, 'Why don't you make me laugh more? I thought you'd be more fun.'

Brill tried to think of something funny to say. 'I know a riddle,' he finally said.

'Tell me.'

'Although a bird's not one of the sages, he gives wisdom that lasts through the ages.'

The prince frowned. 'That's too hard. Oh, I know, birds give eggs.'

'But eggs turn rotten if you keep them very long. They don't last through the ages.'

'What is it then?' demanded the prince.

'A quill pen. People write wise things that will be read by people yet unborn.'

Prince Grossder wrinkled his nose. 'That's not a funny riddle. I want a *funny* riddle.'

Brill thought of one he had heard when he first started school. 'Who has a trunk but doesn't pack his clothes in it?'

'I know, I know!' cried the prince. 'An elephant.'

'That's right. You're very clever.' Brill realized the best riddles would be simple ones the prince could guess.

Brill racked his brain, trying to remember all the jokes and riddles the kids used to tell at school. He managed to keep the prince laughing as they rode home from the play park. But Brill wondered how he'd keep Grossder amused when he ran out of riddles.

When Brill returned to his room, he found the tailor waiting for him. Brill's new outfit was finished—a dark-blue tunic with light-blue hose. His new shoes were black with curled toes.

The tailor said, 'You'll be a handsome fellow at the emperor's banquet tonight.'

'What banquet?'

'Hasn't anyone told you? Tonight the emperor honours the members of his council. Everyone will be dressed in his best clothes. Come, let's see if the prince is ready to go downstairs.'

Brill followed the tailor. Meopar was placing a jewelled crown on the prince's head. His tunic was brown velvet trimmed with brown fur. Grossder reminded Brill of a giant stuffed bear.

'How do you like my new outfit?' he asked. 'I wanted it to be the colour of chocolate.'

'You look very fine,' said Brill.

'I think state banquets are deadly dull, but I'll try to smile and look happy.' The prince sighed as if no one realized what a hard life he lived.

Brill followed Prince Grossder into the dining hall, where servants were seating people according to rank. They bowed to the prince and escorted him to the head table where Princess Florette was already sitting. Brill was shown to a chair beside Segra near the back of the room.

Segra whispered, 'How are you?'

'My left ankle's sore, but I don't have to do much walking so it's not really a problem. The prince hasn't even noticed my limp.'

'The prince doesn't think about much except himself.'

Brill nodded. 'Thanks for getting that guard's attention. I thought I was a goner when I saw him coming.'

'It was the least I could do after getting you into the mess.'

'What did you tell him?'

'I asked if he had seen Princess Florette's white poodle go by. I had to think fast—to keep the guard from seeing you. We spent quite a bit of time looking for the dog.'

'You're very clever.'

'One has to be to get along here. The princess was peeved when I returned late for breakfast, but she doesn't stay angry long. She's much easier to get along with than Prince Grossder. Whatever made him choose brown for his banquet suit?'

'He wanted it to be chocolate-coloured. He doesn't know he looks like a fat bear.'

Segra muffled a giggle. 'Stand up. Here comes the emperor and the queen.'

Everyone stood and the orchestra played a solemn march. The emperor smiled and nodded as he strutted up the centre aisle to the head table on a raised platform.

Brill enjoyed his dinner. It was a treat to eat fish, beef, vegetables, and fruit that tasted like themselves instead of like chocolate. He thought of the hard-working farmers and fishermen who had produced the food.

After dinner, dancers and jugglers entertained the guests. Finally the emperor stood to make his speech. He warned everyone to watch for rebels.

'I have been very patient all these years, but now the time has come to eliminate every person who is disloyal to the empire.'

The audience clapped loudly as if to affirm that they had no rebellious thoughts.

The emperor continued, 'As you know, I have let Talder live—even though I know there are traitors in our empire who want to go back to the terrible days when he was king. I expect I have been too kind, but now the safety of our empire makes it necessary for Talder to die.

'One month from today is Empire Day when we cele-brate the beginning of our glorious empire. I have decided that would be an appropriate day to throw Talder to the dragators as a signal to all rebels that we will no longer over-look treasonous acts of any kind.'

Everyone applauded. Even Brill and Segra went through the motions of clapping but without enough force to make any sound.

Brill saw the alarm in Segra's blue eyes. As the roar of applause died, she whispered, 'We have to help the king escape.'

'Don't look at me. I never was any good at impossible tasks.'

'We can't let the king die!'

'But there's no way he can escape.' Brill looked around hoping no sharp ears were listening to their whispered comments. 'We can't talk now,' he said.

The next morning Brill went out early to find the man who knew his father. He walked through the orchard several times, but the man was not there. Brill ate a peach and returned to his room. He was glad he hadn't seen Segra. He hoped she realized how impossible it would be to help the king escape.

It was several days later before Brill finally found the man again picking peaches.

'Sir, do you have time to tell me where Stronall is?' Brill asked.

The man looked around to see if anyone could hear their conversation. 'Stronall was executed as a rebel,' he whispered.

Brill shivered. 'Dragators?'

The man nodded. 'They caught one rebel and tortured him until he confessed to a plot to kill the emperor and release Talder.'

'How long ago?'

'Almost two years, I think. The rebels have been lying low since then. Do not admit to anyone you're Stronall's son. He was the leader. Brave fellow.'

Brill rushed back to his room where he could be alone to cry. His father had been brave to plot against the emperor. If only he could be that brave, but he was so afraid of the dragators.

He was too sad to think up anything funny that day, and the prince complained, 'Why don't you make me laugh today?'

'Let's go to the library and find a funny book. I'll read to you.'

'You go and bring back something funny. I'm going to order some chocolate pudding. I'm hungry.'

When Brill went to the library, he found Segra. 'Where's the princess?'

'She's having her hair done so I have a little time to myself.'

Brill exclaimed, 'I didn't know there were so many books.'

'King Talder collected them. He hired scribes to go to other countries to copy their books.'

Brill walked along the shelves looking at the titles tooled* on the leather bindings.

Segra said, 'Tell me if you see anything about mountain climbing. I might be able to use the techniques to help the king get out of his courtyard.'

'Even if he got out, he couldn't get off the island. There are soldiers everywhere.'

'But I can't let him die. I've been giving him food, and he's getting stronger.'

'How are you getting the food to him?'

'I push peanuts, grapes, and bits of cheese through the small hole in the wall.'

'Segra, I have just found out that my father died trying to help the king. If a grown man couldn't succeed, how could you?'

Her eyes glistened with tears. 'Oh, Brill, I'm sorry about your father. I should think you'd want to continue his work. I need someone to help me.'

He snapped, 'But it's impossible. Absolutely impossible.' Brill found a book of funny poems. 'I have to get back to the prince.'

He again managed to make the sullen prince laugh as he read to him that afternoon. Brill himself laughed at the silly rhymes, but he longed to be by himself where he could let tears relieve some of his heartache.

The next morning when Brill awoke, he dressed and then pulled the curtains open. He looked down and saw a girl running through the orchard to the garden. Though he couldn't see her face, he guessed it was Segra.

Brill wondered if someone were chasing Segra. Was she in some kind of trouble? Should he go and help her? He didn't really want to get involved in one of her wild schemes, but he didn't want her to be hurt. He looked down again, but she was gone.

Brill sat at his desk and tried to think of a way to amuse Prince Grossder. He was interrupted by an impatient knocking at his door. He opened it, and Segra stepped inside.

She gasped, 'Brill, please come quickly! I need your help.'

He frowned. 'You aren't trying to help the king escape, are you?'

'No, nothing like that. Please hurry,' she begged. 'We won't be helping rebels. I promise you that.'

Brill sighed. The prince wouldn't wake up for another hour or so. 'I'll go—but if this is another of your dangerous schemes, I'm coming back.'

Segra led the way out of the palace, through the garden and orchard, and into the woods. A spine-chilling scream sent goosepimples running down Brill's spine. He stopped.

'Wh—What's that?' he whispered.

'You'll see.'

The scream came again, followed by muffled sobs. It sounded like an animal, yet the suffering behind the cries seemed human. Who was it?

6

Segra's Dangerous Plan

*T*HE CRIES BECAME LOUDER as the children came closer to it. Brill followed Segra.

'What's making that awful noise?' he demanded.

'You'll see.' Segra stopped to pull a rope from a hollow tree. 'Here, you carry this.' She picked up a short branch.

'What are you going to do?' asked Brill, remembering how he barely escaped with his life the last time he had been involved with one of Segra's schemes. His sensible side kept telling him to run back to the palace. 'Segra, I want to know what you're planning.'

'Don't be so nervous. You won't be in any danger.'

But shivers of fear crawled over Brill's skin as another cry of agony pierced the air. The sound was very near.

They came to the end of the forest. Below them lay the deep moat. Brill looked down on a narrow beach where a dragator bellowed in pain.

'I think he has broken his foreleg. I'm going to set it.'

Brill gasped, 'You're out of your mind! Dragators eat people! Remember?'

'He won't eat me. Look at those sad black eyes. He's begging for someone to stop the pain. All I want you to do is hold the rope when I go up and down. Belay* it around that tree.'

'Even if this dragator is friendly, what about all the others?'

'I don't see any others.'

'They may still be sleeping, but soon they'll come looking for their breakfasts.'

'You watch for them. You can warn me if you see one crawling towards me.'

Segra pulled a strip of cloth from her pocket and tore it into ribbons. 'I'm ready. Hold the rope steady.'

'Do you know how to set bones?'

'Father's a doctor. I used to help him.'

Segra tied the rope around her waist and started down the steep cliff wall. Brill lowered the rope as she needed it. He shuddered as he saw the injured dragator watching her.

'Keep away from his fiery breath,' Brill called.

Segra reached the narrow beach. Brill grasped the rope firmly, ready to pull if the dragator tried to eat her. Segra put some peaches by his mouth, and he looked at them curiously as she patted his scaly head.

He probably only eats raw meat, thought Brill.

'I'll have your poor leg better very soon,' Segra said softly. She knelt beside the creature and put the stick next to his leg. Carefully, she felt the bone. The dragator bellowed.

Brill cried, 'Don't hurt him! He won't understand.'

But the huge beast lay still as Segra tied the stick on with the cloth ribbons.

'It won't hurt so much if you keep it perfectly still,' explained Segra as if the beast could understand. 'You'll have to stay quiet while the bone is healing. Please don't try to swim. I'll bring you food. I wish you could tell me what you like.'

As if to answer her, the dragator ate one of the peaches in one gulp, seed and all.

She patted his head. 'I'll bring you more fruit and vegetables from the garden. I have to go now, but I'll be back tomorrow morning. I think I'll call you Peachy.'

He nuzzled his ugly head against her.

Segra signalled Brill to pull her up. She climbed up the steep cliff as he slowly pulled up the rope. He couldn't believe what he had just seen—a dragator who didn't swallow a person when he had a chance.

As Segra came to the top of the cliff, he asked, 'Wasn't his breath burning hot?'

She shook her head. 'Only a little warm.'

'Maybe it only turns hot when he's about to eat somebody.'

'Or else it's been greatly exaggerated.' Segra untied the rope around her waist. 'If Peachy stays quiet, his leg should heal fast.'

Brill said, 'We'd better hurry back to the palace.'

Segra waved good-bye to Peachy. He made a gutteral sound in his throat as if he were swallowing a sob.

Brill coiled the rope, and Segra hid it in the hollow tree.

She followed him through the woods. 'Dragators are not as fierce as people think,' she said.

'They *eat* people,' reminded Brill.

'It's probably because they're starving. I think they'd rather eat fruits and vegetables. If all you had to eat was slimy water plants, you'd get very hungry.'

'I wouldn't eat raw people.'

Segra muffled a giggle. 'Would you eat cooked people?'

'You have a strange sense of humour.'

'I know, but it helps me get through the days.'

Brill opened the palace door, and they slipped inside. He hurried to his room. He was safe. Prince Grossder had not yet awakened.

The amazing events of the morning kept running through Brill's mind. Was Segra right? Did dragators have a gentle side? Or had Peachy eaten Brill's father?

When Brill was called by Grossder, the prince began complaining. 'Today the king of Leoniff is coming with his whole family. I have to greet them when they arrive. I hate Oplack, the crown prince. Last time he was here, he asked why I wore pillows in my clothes.'

'Why didn't you threaten to throw him to the dragators?' asked Brill.

'I wish I could have, but Father says we have to keep on good terms with Leoniff. The fierce warriors of Asperita won't dare attack us if we keep our alliance with Leoniff.'

'How long are your visitors staying?'

'They'll leave tomorrow. After the welcoming ceremony I'm to take Oplack to the play park. You can help me entertain the little monster.'

The day at the play park was hectic. Little Prince Oplack delighted in teasing Prince Grossder.

'You could get a job as the fat man in the circus,' Prince Oplack laughed.

'I am the crown prince of Exitorn, and I shall be emperor,' declared Prince Grossder.

Brill tried to distract the teasing prince. 'Would you like a merry-go-round ride?'

He shrugged. 'I suppose so.'

As they climbed aboard, Prince Oplack ran to the large horse reserved for Prince Grossder. 'I want to ride on *this* one,' he said.

Brill grabbed his hand and pulled him to another horse. 'Here's the finest horse, Prince Oplack. You can lead the parade.'

Prince Grossder waddled over to his special horse, and Meopar helped him on.

Prince Oplack laughed. 'I never knew anyone who was so fat he had to have a special horse built for him.'

Brill mounted another horse as the merry-go-round began to move.

After a couple of turns Prince Oplack yelled, 'Hey, can't this thing go any faster? Or is it too heavy with Prince Grossder aboard?'

Brill tried to think what he could do to silence the cheeky little prince.

Later at the zoo, Grossder decided to stay in the coach while Oplack and Brill walked closer to the animals.

Brill said, 'Good manners are very important for princes.'

'Princes can do whatever they like,' retorted Oplack.

'It is not good manners to make fun of how somebody looks.'

'I can say whatever I want.' Oplack pressed his lips together in a determined expression.

'Someday when you're king and Prince Grossder is emperor, you may need the emperor's help. Grossder will remember how you teased him, and he'll refuse your request.'

'I won't *ever* need his help.'

'Leoniff is smaller than Exitorn. Clever princes are friendly to all rulers, for they never know when they'll need their help.'

'I'm clever.'

'Of course you are, so I know you'll stop teasing Prince Grossder.'

He stuck out his lower lip. 'I was tired of teasing that fat fool anyway.'

Oplack ran ahead and began making grotesque faces at the monkeys who looked at him curiously.

The carriage driver interrupted them. 'Prince Grossder wishes you to join him for lunch.'

'But I haven't finished looking at the animals,' complained Oplack.

'We can come back later,' promised Brill.

They walked to the small restaurant set up for the prince and princess.

Prince Grossder was sitting at a table with Segra and Princess Florette. Brill and Prince Oplack joined them. Grossder had already ordered for them: chocolate-crusted chicken, chocolate milk, and fudge pudding.

Prince Oplack smiled. 'My mother would never let me eat this much chocolate. She makes me eat spinach and liver so that I'll be clever and healthy.' He looked at Prince Grossder. 'I suppose your mother doesn't care if you're clever and healthy.'

Grossder hastily swallowed his mouthful of food and spluttered, 'Chocolate is the most healthy food there is.'

Oplack laughed. 'Ho, ho, ho—are you telling me your mountains of fat are healthy?'

Brill poked Oplack with his elbow to remind him of the danger of teasing Grossder and tried to change the subject. 'What have you girls been doing today?'

Princess Florette answered, 'Watching the puppets. They're my favourite.'

Prince Oplack grinned at her. 'How did you get your hair so red—dip it in cherry juice?'

'My hair grows this way,' snapped Florette.

'She has red hair like fire, so beware of her ire,' chanted Oplack.

The princess broke into tears.

Segra put her arm around her. 'Don't cry, Florette. Your hair is beautiful. Everyone says so, except this unmannerly boy.'

The princess wiped her eyes. 'I'm not crying because of what he said. I'm crying because Father says I have to marry him when I'm fifteen.' She broke into fresh sobs that shook her body.

Prince Grossder announced, 'I shall forbid it. I will not have this nasty boy related to us.'

Oplack retorted, 'Exitorn needs Leoniff as an ally. I don't mind marrying apple-top because I'll probably have to rule Exitorn too. Grossder will be so fat by then, he won't be able to move.'

Prince Grossder stood and shook his finger. 'When I get to be emperor, I'll order my soldiers to march into Leoniff! I'll make it part of my kingdom!'

A look of alarm flashed on Oplack's face. 'I was only joking. I didn't mean it. Florette, your hair is beautiful— and Grossder, eating is a fine hobby. You are so talented in selecting gourmet food.'

The rest of the afternoon Oplack complimented Grossder whenever he had a chance. By the time they returned to the palace, Prince Grossder was in a good mood.

That evening the emperor entertained the visiting royal family at a dinner in the throne room. Brill was not invited, and a maid brought him dinner in his room.

A little later Segra knocked on his door. She was carrying a handkerchief tied around a bundle.

'Brill, will you take this food to the king tomorrow morning? I want to go to the moat to see how Peachy is doing.'

'But how will you get down to the moat without me?'

'I'm not going down unless there's a problem. I'll just drop some cabbages and peaches for him to eat. I don't think he'll mind if they get a bit squashed.'

'I expect I can poke food in to the king,' agreed Brill, feeling creepy fingers of fear tingle his back at the thought of being caught. He asked, 'Segra, why are you so brave?'

'I'm not brave.'

'Yes, you are. You help the king even though you know it's dangerous. And you helped the dragator who might have eaten you. I wish I were brave like you.'

Segra looked thoughtful. 'Do you remember the war with Asperita three years ago?'

'Yes. We were afraid the Asperitans would invade our village, but the emperor's soldiers drove them back.'

'The Asperitans climbed our mountain. I suppose they wanted to use it for a lookout point. We saw them coming, and we escaped down the other side. It was very frightening. We moved at night and hid in caves in the daytime.'

'Did they catch you?'

'No, but almost. One of the women from our settlement had a fretful baby. He cried most of the time. As the soldiers got closer, our headman said she'd have to leave the child or we'd all be captured. The parents agreed, but my father said he'd stay and care for the baby.'

'What did you do?'

'Mother and I stayed with Father while the rest of the people fled.'

'Did the Asperitans find you?'

'No, the baby finally fell asleep, and the soldiers passed by our cave.'

'Weren't you terribly scared?'

'Yes, but Father said, "If you love Jesus with all your heart, you belong to Him for all eternity. You don't have to be afraid of anything." I've never forgotten those words. A few days later the war ended, and we went home.'

'Aren't you afraid of getting hurt? When you went down by the moat, weren't you scared of getting bitten by the dragator's sharp teeth or burned by his fiery breath?' Brill asked.

'I think I was concentrating so hard on how I could tend his leg, I forgot the danger.'

Segra ran her fingers through her blonde hair. 'Brill, we must help the king escape. In three weeks there'll be a full moon, and that should give us enough light.'

'But Talder is too feeble to even climb out of his courtyard.'

'That's why it's important to keep giving him more food.'

'Even if he gets out of prison, how will he escape from the island?'

'If Peachy's foreleg heals, I'll try to ride him across the moat. If he gets used to a rider, we'll be able to put the king on his back.'

'Are you out of your mind? This is the wildest idea you've had yet!'

'It's the only way. It might work. We *have* to try.'

Brill scowled. 'Even if the king gets across the moat, how will he get up on the other side?'

'I haven't worked that out yet.'

Brill shook his head. 'There's not a chance in the world that your plan will work. Even if Peachy lets you ride him, how can you be sure he'll be there when you need him or that he'll let the king ride him?'

'I know you won't believe it, but I think Peachy understands me. I'm going to tell him how important he is to my plan.'

Brill shook his head. 'Peachy may be friendly to you because you tended his leg, but he isn't clever enough to understand his part in the king's escape. Please forget your plan and stay out of trouble.'

'I can't do that. There's no one else to help the king,' Segra replied. Then she left.

Later that night as he crawled into bed, Brill prayed, 'Dear Lord, help me to be brave so that I can do what you want me to do. Grandfather said you love us, but I'm so scared. I'd like to help the king escape, but I don't want to go to prison. I wish I could convince Segra to be more careful. She's brave, but she's reckless—and that could get us both fed to the dragators.'

Brill finally fell asleep. He dreamed Prince Grossder was pushing him into the moat where dragators awaited with open jaws. He woke up in a cold sweat.

The next morning Brill went through the forest to the prison. He waited until the guard passed, and then he slipped up to the wall and began poking peanuts, grapes, and pieces of cheese through to the other side. With a hammering heart, he kept watching for the guard.

He heard a cracked voice say, 'Thank you, Segra.'

'It's Brill today. I'm the boy who fell into your courtyard.'

'Thank you, Brill. Is Segra all right?'

'Oh yes. She's taking some food to an injured dragator.'

The voice laughed, then grew solemn. 'You're probably helping to feed the dragators too. They tell me I'm scheduled to be a dragator meal on Empire Day.'

'Segra has a plan to help you escape. I'm bringing you extra food so you'll be strong enough to climb out of your courtyard.'

'You must tell Segra not to risk her life for me. I've lived a fine life. I don't mind going to meet my Maker.'

'I'll tell Segra.'

'Someday Exitorn will again have a ruler who cares about the people. I hope it will be my son, but no one even knows if he's alive. He left long ago to live among the people so that he would understand their problems when he became king.'

'It sounds as if he'd be a great king.' Brill pushed in the last of the food. 'I'd better go now. I'll see you later.'

Brill breathed a sigh of relief as he reached the safety of the woods.

For the next two weeks Brill continued to give food to the king. He didn't eat all of his own meals but saved the small things—bits of chocolate, raisins, cherries, almonds, cashews, and sunflower seeds. He found that thin carrots, cherry tomatoes, and peapods from the palace garden would fit in the small hole in the wall.

In the meantime, Segra reported she had tied her rope to a sturdy tree, and she was able to climb up and down the cliff to the narrow beach. Peachy's foreleg had healed enough so that he could swim again. He met her eagerly each morning to see what she brought him from the garden.

As Segra met Brill one morning in the forest, she exclaimed, 'Brill, you're not going to believe this, but I told Peachy about the king needing to ride on his back. It looked as if he understood me. When I asked him if I could ride, he slipped into the water and waited for me to get on. Then he swam across to the other side and back.'

'You actually *rode* him?'

'Yes, and apart from getting my feet and legs all wet, it worked out fine.'

'But what if another dragator decides to eat one of your legs? Don't you see the danger you're in?'

'Other dragators were swimming nearby. They didn't bother me.'

'Dragators *eat* people! It's not safe to be riding around in that moat even if Peachy is friendly.'

But as usual Segra didn't pay any attention to Brill. 'The night of the full moon comes in six days. I'll have to borrow another rope from the groundskeeper's shed.'

'What for?'

'I'm going to throw it around a tree on the other side of the moat—so the king will have something to climb up.'

'It won't be easy to throw a rope around a tree at the top of the bank.'

'I know, but I have to do it.'

'There are so many things that can go wrong,' muttered Brill.

'But there's a chance that everything will go right. I have to take that chance. You'll help me, won't you, Brill?'

'I suppose I'll have to. You can't do it alone.' But Brill's stomach tightened in a painful knot.

7

Disaster!

ON THE DAY of the planned escape, Brill arose before dawn and went out to meet Segra. Dew lay heavily on the grass and shrubs. The air was bitterly cold. The eastern sky began to show light as Segra and Brill walked quietly through the forest to the spot where they had first seen Peachy.

Peachy was there, but another larger dragator lay beside him. Brill whispered, 'We can't go down there now, Peachy has company.'

'This is the only time we have. I'll go if you've changed your mind.'

'You said you tried to throw the rope yesterday, but it wouldn't catch on the tree. I have to go.' Brill sighed, wondering again why he had let himself get involved in Segra's dangerous plan. 'I wish I had a sword.'

'You can't chop up one of Peachy's friends,' cried Segra. 'Swords don't solve problems. They only create worse ones.'

Segra climbed down the rope. Peachy waddled towards her, rubbing his scaly head against her legs. Segra took the produce from her sack—cabbages, carrots, and his favourite—peaches.

Brill watched the other dragator warily. He wished he knew what was going on in his small reptile brain. As Brill descended the rope, Segra tossed food to the other dragator. He chomped on it eagerly. Brill didn't like his pointed teeth.

Segra knelt beside Peachy, talking to him as if he could understand. 'I want you to take Brill across the moat. He's going to throw a rope around a tree on the far bank, so the king can climb up the other side. Tonight is the night of the escape—remember?'

'He can't understand,' Brill interrupted. 'Come on, let's get it over with.'

Brill took off his shoes and stockings and put the coil of rope over one shoulder. He forced his mind to concentrate on the details of what he was doing rather than on the dangers.

Peachy slipped into the water and waited by the shore. Brill climbed on his back.

'Squeeze your knees against his body. That'll hold you on,' advised Segra.

Brill nodded. The water felt icy cold on his bare feet and legs. Brill couldn't tell how much of his shivering was from the cold and how much was from fear. Peachy's sharp scales scratched his bare skin. But the thought of other dragators cruising along looking for breakfast bothered him the most.

Peachy headed straight across the moat and stopped by a ledge on the other side. Brill hopped off. He had tied the rope in a lasso, and he threw it towards the tree he and Segra had agreed looked the strongest. He missed. Again and again he threw and missed. His arm ached from the effort. Perspiration ran down his face.

'I'll be ready in a minute,' he called to Peachy. *Now I'm doing it,* he thought. *Talking to that stupid dragator just as if he can understand me. But how did he know where to take me? And how does he know to wait for me?*

Brill pushed the puzzling questions from his mind and threw the lasso once more. It caught on the tree, and Brill pulled it tight.

He climbed a little way up the bank to be sure the rope would hold. It seemed firm. Excitement burst in Brill's mind as an idea came. Why didn't he go with the king? He'd need someone to help him. They could hide near his mother's farm. He longed to see his mother again. A happy picture flashed in his mind—he was sitting by the fireplace telling his mother about his adventures.

Brill dropped back to the beach, satisfied the rope was secure. He climbed on Peachy's back, patted his scaly head, and said, 'Good job.'

Peachy swam towards the other side, but as they came to the middle of the moat, Brill saw three large dragators swimmimg towards them. The one in the lead opened his mouth and bellowed. Brill crouched low on Peachy's back. If only they could reach the shore before the dragators began chewing on his bare legs.

'Hurry, Peachy,' he whispered.

The lead dragator swam fast, and he came up beside them, looking up at Brill.

He doesn't look as if he'll be satisfied with my leg. He wants all of me. If I still had my rope, I'd lasso him and tie his mouth shut. I don't have any way to defend myself. Dear God, please help me! You're the only One who can.

The three dragators closed in on Peachy, and Brill braced himself for the pain of sharp teeth biting his flesh and crunching his bones. He would scream and shout, and

Segra would see he was not brave at all. But it wouldn't matter what she thought after he was dead.

They came closer to shore, and still the dragators had not bitten him. Brill began to hope. Perhaps the strange dragators knew he was Peachy's friend.

Peachy stopped by the beach, and Brill scrambled onto dry land. He grabbed his shoes and stockings, rushed to the rope, and climbed up. Segra was sitting at the top of the bank waiting for him.

'It all worked out perfectly!' she exclaimed.

'Oh yes.' Brill sat down beside her to put on his shoes. 'I only got scared out of my wits by those big dragators following us back.'

'But they didn't hurt you.'

'No. Maybe they weren't hungry. But my heart is still beating like a drum. I expected to feel teeth any minute.'

'The other dragators never bothered me when I rode Peachy,' said Segra. 'We'd better get back to the palace.'

As they walked Brill said, 'Let me tell you my idea. I've decided to escape with the king. He'll need someone to help him, so I'm going too.'

'We can ask the king if he wants a companion.' Segra's eyes sparkled. 'A king should have two servants. We'll both go. It would be wonderful to see my parents again.'

'Great idea.'

Segra was silent for a minute, then her face clouded. 'I'm afraid it will make things too complicated. Peachy can only carry one person at a time, and it will take too long to get us all across the moat. Let's wait and go another night. Nothing must interfere with the king's escape.'

Brill frowned. 'Now that I've started thinking about going home, I can't bear to stay here.'

'I'll pray that God will help us know what He wants us to do.'

They returned to the palace.

After breakfast Prince Grossder and Brill went to the play park. The prince complained, 'What's the matter with you, Brill? You act as if your mind is a million miles away.'

'I was trying to think of some new games for us to play.'

'What kind?'

'Guessing games—the kind you're so good at.'

'I'm bored with this silly play park. Let's go back to the palace.'

Brill found it hard to think about amusing the prince when his mind was so full of plans for going home. He hoped he could convince the king to take him along, but if not he'd go the next night. He imagined walking into his house, surprising his mother and grandfather. He could hide in the cave under Black Rock until the emperor's soldiers gave up looking for him.

'Brill! Why aren't you listening to me?' shouted the prince.

'Uh, sorry, your highness. I was just trying to think of some riddles for my new game.'

'But if you make it up, you'll know all the answers, and you'll beat me,' pointed out Grossder.

'I could never win playing against you, your highness. With your genius-level intelligence, no one can beat you. I wish I were half as clever as you.' Brill had learned that a liberal dose of flattery could always soothe the prince's rumpled feelings.

The day dragged by. Finally the prince announced that he was going to bed, and Brill escaped into his bedroom.

He opened his curtains. When the moon was high in the sky, he and Segra planned to slip out of the palace. Brill tried to swallow the sour taste that came from his scared stomach.

Brill took off his clothes and put on his homespun tunic. It felt much scratchier than he remembered. Over his homespuns he put on his palace clothes. He'd be ready to leave if he got the chance. He couldn't walk down a road with his bright coloured silk clothes without attracting attention.

The full moon rode high in the sky, and Brill guessed it was close to midnight. Hopefully everyone in the palace was asleep except for a few guards. He left his room and glided down to the small door opening to the garden. He looked around, didn't see anyone, and hurried through the garden and orchard, stumbling a couple of times on tree roots. He picked a couple of peaches for Peachy. Without his help, their plan couldn't succeed.

Brill found Segra hiding in the woods near the prison.

'I just saw the guard make his rounds,' she whispered. 'Now is the time to move.' They crossed the clearing around the prison.

Brill climbed the tree, tied the rope around the trunk, and lowered it to the courtyard. The king had placed his bench near the tree, and he climbed on it. He tied the rope around his waist and began climbing the wall, depending on the rope which Brill held taut. He grabbed a tree branch, and Brill reached down to take his hand. Silently Brill guided him to the top of the wall. With the help of tree branches and the rope, the king climbed down to freedom. Brill untied the rope from the tree and dropped beside him. Brill coiled the rope as Segra led the way to the woods.

When they were away from the prison, Segra spoke, 'We've made it this far. Now all you have to do, your majesty, is get across the moat.'

'Are you sure this dragator is reliable?' he asked.

'Peachy has taken both Brill and me for rides,' answered Segra.

Brill felt his heart pounding as he asked his important question. 'Would you like me to come with you?'

'It would be wonderful to have your company,' replied the king, 'but if they caught us, it would mean your execution. I can't let that happen.'

'But I could help you watch for soldiers.'

'It's best that I go alone. One person can hide easier than two.'

Brill pouted. 'But I could look for food for you.'

Segra spoke sharply. 'There's no time to argue now, Brill. We have to do what King Talder thinks is best.' She handed the king a sack. 'Here's some food.'

The king smiled his gratitude and tied the cloth sack to his belt.

Brill said, 'Segra and I will escape tomorrow night. Maybe we'll find you.'

Segra shook her head. 'I've changed my mind. When the king collects an army of rebels, he'll need someone he can trust in the palace. I'll stay here.'

'You're a very brave girl,' said the king. 'You're both brave,' he added.

At the moat, they looked down to see Peachy sleeping on the narrow beach.

Segra asked, 'Your majesty, will anyone know you're gone before morning?'

'I hope not, but sometimes the interrogators* come in the night. They have this strange idea that I know where a treasure is hidden. I suppose they think I'll tell them things when I'm half-asleep that I wouldn't tell them when I'm fully awake.'

'You never know when they're coming?' asked Segra.

'No. But they haven't been bothering me much lately.'

Segra turned to Brill. 'Would you climb that maple tree? From there you can see if anything unusual occurs at the prison.'

Brill nodded. 'If I call *Hurry,* you'll know I see soldiers. If I call, *Danger,* it means they're heading this way.'

Brill climbed the tree and found a fat limb to sit on. He was well hidden by the leaves, but he had a good view of the moat. Segra and King Talder climbed down the rope towards the water. Brill noticed how slowly the king moved. How was he going to keep away from the soldiers who would be sent to search for him? He was too old to run.

Segra woke up Peachy and fed him a peach. It was all up to the dragator now. Brill glanced towards the prison. Burning torches moved about the grounds. Brill's heart pounded. Had they discovered the king's escape?

'Hurry!' he called.

Segra talked to Peachy, and he moved to the water. The king climbed on his back and Peachy swam. Brill saw more torches around the prison. Figures were fanning out through the woods. Some were running along the moat. They'd see the king!

'Danger! Danger!' Brill shouted. Why didn't Peachy swim faster? Why didn't Segra climb up the rope?

The soldiers were coming closer.

'Hide, Segra! Hide!' screamed Brill. But there was nowhere to hide on the narrow beach.

Brill saw more soldiers with torches across the moat. The king wouldn't have a chance to escape.

Brill looked at Peachy silhouetted against the moon-washed water. He had reached the middle of the moat with the king. He wouldn't know that all those torches meant danger.

Peachy dived under the water. *Oh no! That stupid Peachy doesn't know that human beings can't stay under water as long as he can. He's going to drown the king!* Brill closed his eyes in horror.

Then Brill heard soldiers calling to one another near his tree.

'I saw him—out in the water.'

'Swimming across, eh?'

'No, he was riding on a dragator!'

'You've been drinking too much wine.'

'I *saw* them—but now they're both gone.'

'If Talder escapes, the dragators will get fat on soldiers.'

'He won't escape. The dragators eat anything that lands in that moat.'

'Hey, look! There's a girl down there.'

'Where?'

'In the shadow of the cliff, trying to hide.'

'There's a rope . . . . Hey girl, come on up. We want to ask you some questions.'

Brill felt paralyzed in his tree. There were ten soldiers below him, all armed with spears. If only he had a sword, but even so he couldn't fight ten men.

He watched as Segra dived into the moat. One of the soldiers cursed and climbed down the rope. Another followed. They jumped in after Segra.

Brill wished Peachy would come back. He'd scare the soldiers and rescue Segra.

But Peachy didn't appear. The soldiers grabbed Segra, and hauled her kicking and screaming back to the shore. Roughly they bound her hands and feet and carried her to the prison.

Brill thought, *If I stay free, I can help her escape, and we can go home together.* But he had a terrible fear that when the emperor heard of her treachery, he would order her thrown in the moat.

The attempted escape had been a complete disaster. Peachy had drowned the king, and Segra had been captured. Brill had to help her escape before she was executed. But how could he accomplish such an impossible task by himself?

8

New Prisoner

WHEN THE EASTERN SKY began to lighten, Brill climbed down from his tree. Blood rushed to his cramped legs, causing prickles of pain. He walked through the forest, carefully eluding the soldiers who were still searching for the king. As he walked through the orchard, he picked two peaches though the knot in his stomach had taken away his usual morning hunger.

He hoped no one had noticed his absence. A guard stationed at the garden door demanded, 'What are you doing here?'

'I was just getting my morning peaches.'

'I didn't see you come out.'

'I used the door by the kitchen.'

The guard looked at Brill and scowled.

'The prince will be angry if I'm not there when he wakes up,' pleaded Brill.

The guard said, 'You can go in.'

Brill hurried to his room. He quickly took off his clothes, hid his homespuns, and put on clean palace clothes.

Later Grossder summoned him, the prince's eyes glistening with excitement. 'Right after breakfast I want to go to the throne room. Meopar says Talder escaped from prison last night. If he tries to lead a rebellion, there'll be war until every rebel is killed. Isn't that exciting?'

'How could he escape?' asked Brill.

'I don't know. We'll hear more details from Father. I'm glad we get a little excitement once in a while to break the monotony. The people who helped the king will all be executed, and that's fun to watch.'

Brill thought of Segra and shuddered.

In the throne room an unhappy Emperor Immane waved his fat arms as he discussed the situation with his council, who sat in a half circle of chairs around his throne.

'Don't you see what this means? We have rebels right here on Palatial Island. I thought we had killed them all during that last purge. I can't trust anyone!'

One council member stood and bowed. 'Your majesty, it appears that the old king was helped by a young girl who is now under arrest. Surely we have nothing to fear from her.'

The emperor snapped, 'You can be sure she didn't plan the escape. There must have been some men involved, but they all got away.'

'Surely she can be made to reveal the names of the others,' the council member said.

'Yes, yes, of course. I'll find out the names.' The emperor smiled at the thought.

Brill shivered. He felt sick at the thought of what they might do to make her talk. He *had* to help Segra escape, but how? The prison guards would be much more alert after the escape of their most famous prisoner.

The emperor announced, 'Soldiers throughout the empire are on full alert. We have nothing to fear.'

Another council member stood. 'Your majesty, do you have definite word on what happened to Talder?'

'Oh, didn't I tell you?' An evil smile twisted the emperor's face. 'This is the best news of all. We recaptured the king. He will be executed on Empire Day as planned.'

The council cheered.

Prince Grossder leaned over to Brill. 'I'm glad to hear that. We'll have a great celebration after all.'

Brill nodded absently. The emperor must be lying. He had seen Peachy dive under the water with the king. Brill had a good view from his tree. He would have seen if Peachy had surfaced again. Brill was sure the king had drowned, so who was the emperor planning to throw to the dragators on Empire Day?

Emperor Immane dismissed his council. As soon as they were gone, Princess Florette ran up to the throne, tears running down her cheeks. 'Please, Father, don't kill Segra. She's my best friend.'

'Segra is a traitor, my dear. She must die!'

Florette began to cry louder. 'I love Segra. She wouldn't hurt anyone. It's all a mistake. Oh please, let me see Segra. I'm sure she'll be able to explain it all.'

The exalted emperor spoke sternly. 'Florette, I cannot allow traitors to live. Don't you realize how we have to constantly fight against rebels who want to kill us?'

'But Segra wouldn't—'

The emperor roared, 'Segra helped Talder escape! This is the man who wants to take over my empire. Segra *must* die! We'll send scouts out to find another companion for you.'

Florette pouted. 'Nobody will be as much fun as Segra.'

Prince Grossder waddled up to the throne. 'Father, can Brill and I sit in the front row at the execution? Brill has never seen one.'

'Of course, my son.'

Brill swallowed. He didn't want a front-row seat for an execution.

Early the next morning Brill slipped out of the palace and headed for the prison. He saw that his chances of talking to Segra looked grim. Two guards walked around the prison at fifteen-minute intervals. The tree growing by the courtyard wall had been chopped down. It would never again be used to help anyone escape.

Brill wondered if Segra had been put in the cell where the king had been.

When the guards had passed, he rushed up to the wall and called through the hole, 'Segra, are you there?'

A familiar voice answered, 'I fear no evil, for God has His hand upon me.'

Brill felt a chill from his scalp to his toes. 'Grandfather? What are you doing here?'

'Brill, is that you?'

'Yes, Grandfather. Why did they arrest you?'

'I was teaching some of the village children God's laws. I was following God's will. They arrested me and put me in this cell. When I got here, I heard one of the men say, "He looks just like him with that grey beard and hair." Do you know what they meant?'

Brill's blood turned cold. He had a horrible feeling the emperor had found a substitute for Talder. No one had seen the king for many years, and the emperor had killed most of his relatives and friends. No one would know that Grandfather was not the king. Brill cried, 'Oh, Grandfather, you're in great danger!'

'With the Lord taking care of me I have nothing to fear. If this is the time He wants to call me to heaven, I'm ready. You'd better get away before those guards come back.'

'How's Mother?'

'She's fine.'

'Good-bye, Grandfather.'

Brill ran back to the palace. Empire Day was in four days, and now he had two people to rescue.

The next morning Brill heard a soft knocking on his door. He felt his throat catch. It sounded like Segra's knock, and he hurried to the door, hoping by some miracle he'd find her.

Instead he found Princess Florette, her eyes red from weeping. 'Will you go with me to the prison? I must see Segra, but I'm afraid to go through the woods alone.'

'I'll be glad to go with you, Florette,' Brill answered. 'Here, let me carry your basket.' She handed him a basket full of fruit, nuts, and sweets, and he followed as she marched out the front door. The guards bowed, hiding their surprised looks at seeing her up so early.

Brill walked a couple of paces behind her as they passed through the garden and orchard, and came to the forest path.

'You go first and knock the cobwebs out of the way,' said Florette. 'I'm scared of spiders.'

Brill nodded. 'I'll de-web the path for you.' He thought, *After riding a dragator, I guess a little spider won't scare me. Maybe I am getting braver.*

They marched up to the front entrance of the prison.

The princess announced to the two guards standing on either side of the door, 'I have come to see Segra.'

'No visitors allowed,' snapped one.

Florette's green eyes flashed. 'Do you know who I am?'

He looked at her closely and gasped. 'You're the princess. But what are you doing here?'

'I *must* see Segra.'

The guards looked puzzled. One said, 'You can go in, your highness.'

A guard led them down a dark corridor to a small cell. He unlocked the metal door. They walked through the cell to the tiny walled courtyard where Segra sat.

Florette threw her arms around her. 'Please tell me how you got mixed up in the king's escape. I know you wouldn't do anything wrong.'

'I'm afraid you can't help me. The evidence is too strong.'

'But I love you. I couldn't bear to see you executed.'

Segra blinked back tears. 'Thanks for coming, Florette,' she said in a choked voice.

Florette began to sob. Finally she said, 'I'll keep begging Father to spare your life.'

Brill walked around the courtyard trying to work out how he could help Segra escape. A tunnel under the wall? That would take too long. A ladder against the wall? He'd have to climb to the top of the wall, pull up the ladder, then put it down on the other side. Brill shivered. The guards would be sure to catch him. There was no way to get Segra out of the prison.

Florette looked at him. 'What are you doing?'

'Just waiting while you're talking,' he said.

'Brill, we have to help Segra escape.'

'I don't know how we can do that,' he answered.

At that point the guard opened the cell door. 'It's time to leave, your highness.'

'We'll come again,' Florette whispered.

'Thank you for the basket. I shall enjoy it,' said Segra.

They followed the guard through the cell and out to the corridor. He slammed the door and locked it.

As they walked back through the woods, Florette cried, 'I can't bear to think of poor Segra living in that terrible place with cobwebs and black bugs running around. It was awful!'

'Segra is very brave,' Brill said.

'If we could help her escape, she could go home to her mountain. I know Father wouldn't let her be my companion any more, but I want to get her out of that cell. Please help me think of a way.'

'I'll try,' promised Brill.

After breakfast Prince Grossder decided to go to the play park. All Brill wanted to do was sit alone and think of some way to help Segra and his grandfather escape. It wasn't enough to be brave. He had to make his brain think up a foolproof plan. The last escape plan had only made things worse. It was hard to think with Prince Grossder chattering and expecting witty replies.

'Oh look,' said the prince as his carriage pulled away from the palace. 'There comes the execution squad with the prisoner.' He called to the driver. 'Stop, I want to watch.'

Eight soldiers marched along the road. Walking between them and held securely by two soldiers was Brill's grandfather. He walked with his head held high.

Brill swallowed the lump in his throat. 'They shouldn't need all those soldiers to guard one old man.'

'Hey, remember he almost got away. There might be rebels around.'

'Where are they taking him?'

'To the dungeon under the palace. Nobody has *ever* escaped from there. Soldiers will watch him day and night until he's thrown to the dragators.'

As the soldiers passed the carriage, Brill heard his grandfather say, 'We are all imprisoned by evil until we accept Christ whose love sets us free.' Then he looked up and saw Brill. He smiled as if to say, *I'm fine.*

Brill's helplessness clamped like a cruel hand squeezing his heart.

Prince Grossder jeered, 'You'll make a tasty lunch for the dragators, you rebel king!'

Before Grandfather could answer, the soldiers had hurried him towards the palace.

The prince motioned for the carriage to move.

Brill wondered what would happen if he stood up at the execution and shouted that they were executing his grandfather and not King Talder. Even that wouldn't stop the execution. He'd only be denounced as a liar.

As they came to the play park, the prince complained, 'You're no fun today. You had better stop looking so miserable, or I'll find a new companion.'

Brill heard the threat, but it failed to scare him. He couldn't see any ray of hope in a life which continued to bring new disasters each day.

As he lay in bed that night, Brill decided that the best thing to do was run away. He'd go the night before Empire Day, because people would be too busy celebrating the next day to look for him. That way he wouldn't have to watch his grandfather being thrown to the dragators. Even the thought of it made him sick. He couldn't bear to be there. His mother needed him now that grandfather was no longer there to help. He thought longingly of hiding in one of the hill caves near the farm. His mother would bring him food. He'd be safe then—unless someone suspected his mother and followed her. What if they arrested her too?

'Lord, help me to do what is best—not only for me, but for those I love. I don't want to put Mother in danger. I'd like to help Segra, but I can't think of a way. Please help me know what you want me to do.'

The night before Empire Day, Brill slipped out of the palace, picked up peaches for Peachy, and walked through the woods. Peachy was sleeping in his usual place. But as Brill looked down, an idea came to him of how to rescue Segra. He argued with himself.

'Don't go back now. Not when you have a way to escape.'

'I can't leave Segra if there's a chance to help her.'

'It won't work. I'll be in too much danger.'

'I know it's risky, but I have to try. I just have to.' Brill tossed the peaches to Peachy, and went back to the palace.

He needed to see Florette, for the plan depended on her, but there was no time the next morning. When he woke up, he found that an excited Grossder was already awake, and Brill couldn't slip away.

After breakfast Prince Grossder's excitement grew. 'Come on, Brill, let's go to our seats for the parade and execution.'

Brill said, 'I don't feel very good. I think I'll stay here.'

'You can't miss the biggest event of the year. You'll feel better when you see all the fancy costumes in the parade. I want you to come,' Grossder said in the stubborn tone that would not allow any argument.

Brill walked behind him. He couldn't bear to watch the execution, but what choice did he have? He concentrated on plans for Segra's escape.

The prince slowly climbed the stairs of the reviewing stand. He grasped the railing to help lift his great bulk up each stair. They sat in upholstered chairs which provided a perfect view of the drawbridge and the moat below.

Princess Florette was already there. She said mournfully, 'I wish Segra were here.'

Prince Grossder laughed. 'Don't feel bad, Florette. Segra will be the star of our next execution.'

'You're horrid, simply horrid!' Florette began to sob.

As the parade began, Brill saw dancers in colourful costumes and heard bands playing lively music. Each unit stopped in front of the emperor's stand. Jugglers threw balls around, and horsemen did tricks on their decorated horses. Many marchers carried signs that read, *Long Live Our Exalted Emperor*.

Brill couldn't enjoy the spectacle. He could only think that each minute brought the execution closer. In the moat several dragators gathered, apparently curious about the music.

Brill tried to watch the parade entertainers, but his eyes kept turning back to the hungry dragators.

At the tail of the parade, a man began to beat a large drum. More dragators swam up.

Apparently, they knew what the drum meant. The creatures crowded under the bridge, shoving and snapping at one another with their sharp teeth. Some stretched their scaly necks from the water and opened their sharp-toothed mouths.

The crowd on the far side of the moat pushed and shoved to see the dragators better.

Prince Grossder nudged Brill. 'Look at that big one with the jagged teeth. I hope he gets the king.'

Brill's heart pounded as rapidly as the frenzied drumbeats. He saw eight soldiers approaching with his grandfather. Nothing could save him now!

9
Prison Visit

THE SOLDIERS MARCHED Brill's grandfather to the centre of the drawbridge.

Grandfather called, 'Turn away from your evil ways and turn to Christ who gave His life for you!'

Emperor Immane stood and waved his arms wildly. 'May this rebel's death be a lesson to all of you! EVERYONE who rebels against ME will die!'

Two soldiers picked up Brill's grandfather as he cried, 'They who rebel against God are lost for eternity!'

They hurled him into the moat. A dragator's large jaws clamped on his frail body and pulled him under the water. It happened so fast that Brill hardly realized it was all over.

Prince Grossder pouted. 'I wish the dragators would eat the people on the surface so we could watch, but they always drag them under. Maybe it's easier to get them away from the other dragators that way.'

Brill blinked back tears. He felt as if someone had kicked him in the stomach, and the ache radiated through his body. His grandfather had been so brave, using his last breath to tell people about God.

If only I'd listened more closely to Grandfather when I was at home, thought Brill. *Maybe I'd be that brave. Then I wouldn't be so scared to try to help Segra. Grandfather said God loved me and He'd stay close to me.*

Brill prayed silently. *Lord, help me to rescue Segra. I need your help because I don't know if my plan will work and I'm not brave.*

Grossder nudged him. 'Come on, Brill. Let's go to the palace for the Empire Day banquet.'

Brill followed him as the royal family walked to the palace dining hall.

As everyone sat down, Emperor Immane raised his wine glass for a toast. 'Here's to the glorious future where every secret rebel will be eliminated. My loyal subjects will all work to make the empire great.'

Brill, who sat near the foot of the long table, thought, *The empire can never be safe or great as long as most of the people are poor and unhappy.*

Servants brought in serving dishes filled with all sorts of foods.

Brill went through the motions of lifting his fork to his mouth, but he couldn't eat much. He thought of his grandfather beyond earthly help and Segra, who still needed his help.

The parade entertainers returned to dance and do magic tricks and acrobatics.

Brill noticed that Florette, sitting by the queen at the head of the T-shaped table, still looked sad. She didn't join in the laughter when two clowns began a mime routine. Brill needed to talk to her, but there hadn't been a chance.

As the evening wore on, the emperor and many of his guests began to show the effects of too much wine. Brill saw Florette leave the head table. Brill too slipped out and caught up with her on the stairway leading to the second floor.

He whispered, 'Florette, I have a plan to save Segra— but I need your help.'

'Me? What could I do?'

'You're about the same size as Segra. We could go and see her, and you two could change places. You should wear a cloak with a hood, and then swap clothes with Segra. That way no one will see that your red hair has turned to blonde when Segra escapes wearing your clothes. I'll tie you up so you won't be blamed.'

Florette's eyes widened in alarm. 'But what if bugs crawl on me?'

'I'll step on all the bugs before I leave you.'

'I want to help; that cell is so smelly and horrible, I cry every time I think of Segra locked in there. How long would I have to stay?'

'Long enough so that Segra and I can escape to the city.'

'Are you going too?'

'My life won't be worth much here if I help Segra escape.'

'I'll have to think about it.' The princess leaned against the gold banister.

'We don't have much time. They'll soon move Segra to the palace dungeon. No one escapes from there.'

'I know.' Florette closed her eyes as if she wanted Brill and his dangerous idea to disappear.

'How do your servants get by the guards at the draw-bridge when you send them to buy something in the city?'

'I give them a pass.'

'Can you get fake passes for Segra and me?'

She nodded. 'Then you could just walk away. Oh Brill, I hope it works.'

'Then you'll help me?'

She hesitated. 'I've never done anything brave before. Oh, I hope the bugs don't crawl on me. I can't stand bugs.'

'We'll go tomorrow morning. What time do you usually wake up?'

'A lot earlier than my lazy brother.'

'Good. Meet me in the garden as soon as you get up.'

Florette whispered, 'I'll be there with the passes.'

She left, and Brill returned to his room. Tomorrow at this time he'd be free, walking towards home. He and Segra would have to hide in the daytime and walk at night. They could cut across fields and avoid the roads. He kept concentrating on the details of his plan, trying to ignore the fear that made his nerves twitch and long for action. The waiting was the hardest. It was impossible to turn off his imagination which kept flashing pictures of soldiers pushing him into a cell or of Grossder laughing as he was thrown to the dragators.

The next day Brill arose early and put on his home-spuns under his palace clothes. He looked out the window to see heavy rain, so he picked out a black cape left by the prince's former companion. Excitement about seeing his mother again mingled with fear at his great danger. Worries marched like an army through his mind. Could he find his way back to his village? What would he and Segra eat? How would they keep away from the soldiers the emperor would send after them?

Brill slipped out of the palace into the garden. He didn't see Florette, so he walked into the orchard and picked a peach. His stomach felt like a hollow gourd, and he hoped the peach would relieve the emptiness. But the gnawing feeling was from fear, and the peach made his stomach gurgle more.

He paced among the fruit trees. Where was Florette? Was she too scared to come? Brill stood under an apple tree watching the garden door of the palace.

Finally it opened and a small figure in a brown cape stepped out.

Brill ran towards her.

'It's raining,' she complained.

'That's good,' answered Brill. 'The guards won't wonder why you're wearing your hood. Come on, we have to hurry.'

Florette followed him as he hurried towards the woods path. He stopped at a hollow tree and pulled out the rope he had borrowed from the groundskeeper's shed. He slipped it under his tunic.

He glanced at Florette as the wind blew her cloak aside. 'Oh, no!' he cried. 'Why did you wear a dress decorated with jewels?'

'I wanted Segra to have it. She can sell the jewels to buy food on her journey.'

'But how are we going to pose as peasants with Segra in a jewelled dress?'

Florette's chin quivered and her eyes filled with tears. 'I was only trying to help.'

Brill stopped. 'I'm sorry I snapped at you. Don't cry. The dress won't show under the cape. Everything will be fine.'

Florette complained, 'You'll have all the fun while I'm lying in that horrible cell.'

'You're very brave, Florette.'

'Do you really think so?'

'Oh, yes. Segra and I will never forget you.'

Florette wiped her eyes. They walked to the prison and found the same guard they had talked to before. He let them into Segra's cell.

As soon as he was gone, Brill said, 'Segra, you and Florette are going to swap clothes, and you and I are going to walk out of here.'

'What will the emperor do to Florette?' cried Segra.

'We'll make it look as if we forced her to take part in the escape. Hurry, Segra, change clothes before the guard gets back.'

Brill turned his back on the girls and began stamping on bugs.

'You're killing all my friends,' complained Segra.

'I hate bugs,' said the princess.

Segra slipped into Florette's cloak. 'When you don't have anything else to do, you watch anything that moves.'

'Ugh, how awful.' Florette wrinkled her nose.

Brill used his rope to knock down cobwebs, and he stepped on the scurrying spiders.

'The place is debugged,' he announced. 'Could we have the passes to cross the drawbridge?'

Florette pulled them from the pocket of the cloak Segra was now wearing. Each pass bore the emperor's gold seal.

Florette sat in the darkest corner, and Brill tied her hands behind her and her feet together. He pulled out a clean white handkerchief. 'I'll have to put a gag in your mouth. Otherwise the guards will think you should have cried out.'

'No, I can't stand to have that cloth in my mouth. Just put it in my lap. I'll pretend I finally managed to spit it out.'

Segra wet it in her washing water and placed it in Florette's lap.

The cell was dark except for the light that came through the courtyard doorway. Brill felt confident the guard wouldn't notice that the figure in the corner was not Segra.

By the time the guard came, Segra had pulled the hood over her head. She put a handkerchief in front of her face and sobbed.

Brill said, 'Princess, you must not cry for Segra. She's a rebel.' He took her hand. 'Come, we must hurry back to the palace.'

They walked out the main door and broke into a run, following a path that would lead them to the road and the drawbridge.

Brill didn't talk, for he needed all his breath for running. Fear squeezed his lungs and made him short of air.

Segra finally cried, 'Brill, can't we stop a minute? I must be weak from being shut in that cell.'

He stopped. 'I wish Florette had let me gag her. I'm afraid if a spider gets close to her, she'll yell. Come on, we've got to keep going.'

Brill took several steps, then stopped. A squadron of soldiers were marching up the road. He grabbed Segra's hand and pulled her behind a bush.

Brill's heart hammered faster than the soldiers' marching feet. He waited until they were out of sight before he stepped out onto the road again.

Segra whispered, 'I hope they aren't looking for us.'

'Just regular manoeuvres.' Brill declared with more confidence than he felt.

As they rounded a bend in the road, they saw the drawbridge.

'We'll soon be free,' said Brill. 'Walk normally now. We don't want anyone to think we're in a great hurry.'

They stopped at the guardhouse and showed their passes to the sentry.

He glanced at the passes and motioned them on.

They walked onto the wooden drawbridge.

'There's a dragator!' exclaimed Segra. 'It looks like Peachy.'

'Forget Peachy and walk straight ahead.'

Behind them they heard feet and a loud cry. 'Close the drawbridge! There's been a prison escape!'

Brill took Segra's hand and began to run, but he faced a line of eight soldiers, marching straight towards them.

The leader barked, 'Go back! Nobody leaves this island until we've found the prisoner!'

Brill shouted, 'We're on an important mission for the palace!' He waved his pass with the golden crest.

The soldiers kept coming. 'Our orders are to close the drawbridge.'

They shoved Brill and Segra back towards the island. The chains clanked as the bridge attendants pulled up the bridge.

'Head for the woods,' whispered Brill to Segra.

But before he could move, he saw that the leader had his big hand clamped on Segra's shoulder. 'Who are you?' he barked.

'Minto, kitchen maid, going to the city for spices,' she answered.

He pulled the hood from her head. 'This must be the blonde girl we're looking for.'

Brill felt a strong hand grip his shoulder, pushing his flesh down to the bone. 'This was the fellow with her.'

The soldier pulled Segra's cloak aside. 'Look at that dress. Since when does a maid wear dresses with jewels?'

'The princess didn't want it any more. She gave it to me,' explained Segra, but she looked at Brill with despair in her eyes.

Brill felt sick. His careful plan had failed.

The eight soldiers formed two lines of four on either side of Brill and Segra. Two soldiers grabbed Segra's upper arms to lead her. Brill felt the painful pressure of big hands on his upper arms also. The soldiers marched them through the main gate of the palace and straight to the throne room.

Brill and Segra were escorted to the emperor, who glared at them with blazing eyes.

'You have been living in *my* palace, eating food and wearing clothes that *I've* provided. And all the time you were traitors!' He waved his podgy arms. 'I sentence you both to die one month from today!'

10

The Dungeon

*B*RILL FOUGHT THE DIZZINESS that swept over
him. He gulped air, determined not to faint. Then
he heard a scream.

Florette rushed up to the throne. 'Father, *please* don't
throw Segra and Brill to the dragators!'

'How can you defend them after what they did to
you?' roared the emperor.

Florette hung her head. 'It wasn't as it looked. I
helped. I want Segra to be free. I love her. Can't you
understand?'

'No, I can't understand treachery—especially by my
own daughter!'

'Our plan would have worked, but when that big black
spider dropped on me, I screamed. Oh Segra, I'm sorry I
messed things up.'

The emperor stood, waving his chubby arms. 'This
rebel girl has bewitched you, Florette. The sooner she dies,
the sooner you'll forget her. Your next companion will be
one hundred percent loyal to the empire.'

Brill heard a whining voice behind him. 'When do *I* get a new companion?' Prince Grossder asked.

'As soon as we can set up new examinations,' answered the emperor. 'We must devise a way to determine the loyalty of those selected.'

The prince munched on chocolate-covered peanuts. 'It's dull not having a companion, but at least we get to watch another execution. That's always fun.'

'Take the prisoners to the dungeon,' the emperor ordered.

The soldiers left the throne room pushing Segra and Brill.

As they came to the narrow stairs leading to the lower levels of the castle, they had to go in single file. Two soldiers led the way, then came Segra, two more soldiers, then Brill and the rest of the soldiers.

After going down two flights of stairs, they reached the dungeon level. Brill and Segra were shoved into a cold dark room. Mildew grew on the stone walls. They smelled the stale, sweaty odour of people, but no one was in the long, narrow room. Brill shuddered as he realized what had happened to the previous inhabitants.

The soldiers talked loudly in the passageways.

'Do we have to stay in this creepy place?'

'We have got our orders. Four of us will guard them by day, and four by night.'

Another voice added, 'We've got this assignment for a month—until they feed the kids to the dragators.'

'I don't know why they assigned four guards to watch two children. They can't escape.'

Brill sat beside Segra on a rough wooden bench, the only piece of furniture in the cell.

Segra said, 'I hope Peachy gets me. He won't let the other dragators eat me.'

'I'm sure he'll protect you.' Brill didn't remind Segra that Peachy had drowned King Talder.

'I'm not scared of dying,' said Segra. 'My father says our souls belong to God. Death isn't the end.'

Brill nodded. 'That's what Grandfather said too.'

'But I'm scared about being thrown off that draw-bridge. The dragators have very sharp teeth.'

'Peachy won't bite you.'

'By now Peachy has probably forgotten me. Let's not talk about dragators. Let's talk about home. What did you like doing the most?'

'Play with the lambs out on the hills.'

'I liked climbing to the top of our mountain where I could look down and see villages that looked like toys. Oh, I'd like to see that view once more.'

Brill tried to blink back the tears that wanted to over-flow his eyes. He longed to go home again, but now that would never be.

Brill began inspecting the walls of the cell.

'What are you doing?' asked Segra.

'Might as well see if there are any loose stones.'

'I'll help. Anything is better than just sitting here.'

Segra stood close to Brill and whispered, 'The soldiers are taking turns watching us. It gives me the creeps to see eyes looking at me as if I'm an animal in the zoo.'

'They can't see much. It's too dark.' Brill ran his hand along the damp and mildewed stones.

'Eeek!' screeched Segra. 'Something furry ran over my foot.'

'A rat?'

'I suppose so. I'm glad you're here,' Segra said, stay-ing close to Brill.

He didn't bother to tell her that rats scared him just as much as they did her.

He found a candle stub, but there was no way to light it.

Brill said, 'Hey, here's a curious thing. At the far end of our cell is a metal wall with a door.'

Segra reached out her hands to touch the wall. 'It *is* metal. I wonder if our cell used to be a hall. It's so long and narrow.'

Brill nodded. 'Maybe it was. I wonder what's behind this door.'

Segra looked back towards the other door. 'I can see eyes watching us.'

'I think it's too dark at this end for them to see us.'

'But you don't know that.'

Brill kept feeling the door. 'I'm going to open it. It doesn't have a lock—just this bar going across to prevent anyone from coming in from the other side.'

'It's not going to be a way to escape. You can be sure of that. They may torture us if they see us trying to open that door.'

'We *have* to try to escape,' insisted Brill. 'You always used to be the brave one.'

'I couldn't stand any more torture.'

'Was it really bad?'

'I don't want to talk about it.'

Brill sighed. 'I won't do anything now, but tonight if everyone's sleeping, we'll try to open the door. I have to know what's on the other side.'

The hours dragged by. Neither ate the watery soup that was stuffed through the door hatch that evening.

Segra said, 'I hope Florette gets a good companion.'

'I feel sorry for Grossder's companion. The prince only thinks of himself.'

'We all have a selfish streak, but most of us grow up enough to realize that we'll be happier if we love other people. That's how God intended us to live.'

Brill nodded, but he wondered why God let Grossder stay alive while he and Segra were about to die.

They didn't sleep that night; the only place to lie down was the cold, dirty stone floor. Brill tried using one of the loose stones for a pillow, but there was no way to be comfortable without blankets or a soft pillow.

Segra sat hugging her knees. 'I don't dare lie down for fear the rats will run over me.'

'We only saw that one. He's probably left to find a place with some spare food. There's nothing around here.'

'I hope you're right.'

Brill kept watching the window in the door waiting for a time when the guards wouldn't be watching, but the eyes didn't leave their post except to change shifts.

They heard when the four soldiers outside their cell were replaced. Brill reckoned it must be morning though no daylight reached their dungeon.

Segra said, 'Breakfast is served,' as two bowls were placed on the sill of the hatch. She handed Brill one of the bowls.

'What is it?' asked Brill as Segra sat beside him on the bench.

'I don't know. Thin porridge maybe.'

'Tastes like liquid straw,' said Brill.

'Don't think I'll eat any.'

Brill pointed out, 'We have to eat something if we're going to survive a month.'

'I'm not going to fatten myself up for the dragators.'

'Segra, you were always the cheerful one. Don't give up yet.'

'It's this place—rats running around, nowhere to sleep, no light. I wish I could die right now.'

Brill whispered, 'Eat something, Segra. If we find a way to escape, you'll have to be strong.'

'Even if that door led to escape, we couldn't go very far because the soldiers would come after us.'

'Our best hope is at night. Last night they kept watching us, but after a while they may become careless. Then we'll open that door.'

Segra ate some of the gruel. 'Tastes like dishwater. By the time they throw us to the dragators, we may be so thin, the dragators will spit us out.'

Brill nodded. 'Then we'll swim to the little beach where we met Peachy and hide until it gets dark. Maybe Peachy will take us across the moat.'

'I wish those eyes would go away. I can't stand being watched all the time.'

Brill took their half-empty bowls back to the hatch. When he returned to the bench, he said, 'It's best not to go near that other door today. We'll pretend we haven't even noticed it.'

That night they slept for a while. Brill shook Segra to wake her. 'I think the guards are asleep. Wake up. Let's try the door.'

Segra sat up, shivering from the cold.

Brill moved quickly and silently towards the door. She followed him.

'Keep watch,' he whispered.

'Nobody's looking at us,' she answered.

Brill felt his heart beating. If only they could get away while the guards slept.

They reached the door. Brill whispered, 'You take one side of the bar, and I'll take the other. We have to lift it off the hooks and put it on the floor without making any noise.'

Segra nodded. She put her hands on the long iron bar.

'Ready?' asked Brill.

'Yes.'

They lifted the heavy bar and lowered it to the stone floor.

Brill grabbed the knob on the metal door and pulled it towards him. It squeaked and he glanced at the window. Still no watchers. He pulled it slowly, hoping the sound wouldn't carry to the guards.

'What's there? It's so dark, I can't see,' whispered Segra.

Brill reached out his hands and felt a dirt wall. He pulled the squeaky door open a little more. 'It's just dirt,' he answered sadly.

'Brill, don't sound so disappointed. You knew they wouldn't give us an easy way to escape.'

'Maybe we can dig a tunnel,' he said.

'How can we do that with guards watching us most of the time? We don't even have anything to dig with.'

Brill pulled the door open wider, and continued feeling, but all he felt was a wall of hard-packed dirt. He pushed the door shut, and Segra helped him replace the bar.

They went back and sat on the narrow wooden bench. Brill spoke in a choked voice. 'Looks as if our only hope is gone.'

Segra said, 'I never was very hopeful. No one ever escaped from the dungeon.'

Brill's face brightened. 'Hey, I know what I can dig with—the iron rod on the door. If I hollow out a place in the dirt big enough for me to stand in, I can dig with the door closed.'

'If there's only one person in this cell, the guards will come marching in to investigate,' pointed out Segra.

'Maybe I can put my cape over some rocks so it will look as if I'm sleeping.'

All day the guards watched them. Brill longed to open the barred door and begin digging. They lay down and tried to sleep. Brill hoped the guards would be too tired to watch them at night. The soldiers were on twelve-hour shifts, and Brill guessed they changed at six at night and six in the morning.

That night Brill and Segra lay in a corner near the observation window and pretended to be asleep. Brill listened to the soldiers' conversation. Most of it didn't interest him, but finally he heard what he had hoped for.

'Hey, Loxer—are the children asleep?'

'Looks like it.'

'It's after midnight. You don't need to watch them while they're sleeping.'

'Those are our orders.'

'Nobody's going to check on us in the middle of the night. You can keep watching until two if you want, but don't wake me up to relieve you. I'm tired.'

Brill lay motionless as if in deep sleep, but he occasionally opened his eyes to peer at the window. Apparently, Loxer had decided not to watch any longer.

Brill whispered, 'Segra, nobody's watching.'

She sat up. 'I think you can start digging. I'll act as lookout.'

They walked to the barred door. Brill felt excited. Perhaps the dirt wall was not thick. Perhaps he could dig his way up to the garden. If only they could escape quickly before the guards realized what they were doing.

He opened the squeaky door and began chipping away at the hard dirt. The bar was not a good digging tool.

Segra kept watch. She spread the loosened dirt around the floor with her hands so no one would notice it.

Some time later she whispered, 'How will we know when it's getting towards morning?'

'You had better go to the other end of the cell and listen to hear if anyone's up.'

'But if they're awake, it will be too late to warn you. They'll see what you're doing.'

'If I could dig a big enough place so that I could close the door, I could keep working.'

'Oh Brill, what if there were a cave-in? You'd suffocate.'

'That's no worse than being eaten by dragators.'

'I think you should stop. You've been at it a long time.'

He argued, 'But I've got so little done.'

'All will be lost if they discover what you're doing.'

Brill pushed his rod into the wall with renewed force loosening more dirt. Perspiration dripped from his face. He stepped back and closed the door. He blew his nose into his handkerchief, trying to remove the dirt particles which were irritating his nostrils.

Segra helped him replace the bar.

They went back and lay down. In a short time they heard the soldiers changing shifts, and bowls of straw-tasting gruel were placed on the ledge.

They both ate, for their stomachs had begun to send strong and desperate hunger messages to their brains.

Brill whispered, 'I keep trying to work out how I can dig more.'

Segra shrugged. 'If that door led anywhere, they wouldn't close it with only a bar on our side.'

'So you think I'm crazy to even make the effort?'

'No, but I'm not going to get my hopes up.'

But Brill was impatient for the day to pass so he could return to his digging. The day shift soldiers kept their eyes on Segra and him every minute.

In the afternoon Brill exercised his legs by walking up and down the long cell. His arms would get their exercise at night. As he came close to the barred door, he stopped. He heard a scratching sound, then a thump.

He shuddered. Probably some sort of animal. A mole maybe. If there were animals, it must mean they weren't too far from the surface. Perhaps he should dig straight up, but he'd need something to stand on. He could stand on the bench so he could reach higher. He kept listening by the door, but all was quiet.

He walked over to Segra and reported the noises on the other side of the door.

Segra sighed. 'I hope it isn't some poor prisoner trying to dig his way to freedom. He'll be very disappointed to see he's dug his way into our cell.'

'I suppose it could be a person digging. I wish I could open that door now.'

'We have to wait until we're not watched.'

'If there are several prisoners, maybe we could over-power the guards, dress in their clothes, and escape.'

'I'd have trouble looking like a soldier.'

'You could cut your long hair.'

'With what?'

'With one of the soldiers' swords.'

'Speaking of swords, remember you'd probably be chopped up before you had a chance to do much. You don't have any weapons.'

'I could hit them on the head with the door bar.'

'How would you get out of our cell?'

'I was hoping the other prisoners might know of a way.'

'My father used to say, "When things look blackest, God is closest."'

'Grandfather said, "Nothing can stop God's plan." He was brave even as he was being thrown to the dragators.' Brill choked back a sob.

Brill walked back to the door. He knocked several times. If another prisoner had dug a tunnel, he might hear and answer, but there was no response.

Brill waited anxiously for night when the watching eyes would disappear, and he could find out what was going on behind the door.

11

Dark Tunnel

BRILL AND SEGRA again pretended to sleep, hoping the guard assigned to watch them would become too tired or bored to stare.

Finally the eyes disappeared, and all was quiet. Brill arose and tiptoed to the barred door. Segra followed him, looking back at the window as she walked.

They lifted the bar, and Brill pulled the door open. He sucked in his breath in surprise. A small tunnel had been dug through the wall of dirt. 'Segra, look!'

She reached out and touched the damp dirt wall of the tunnel. 'Somebody has dug from the other side!'

'That's what I heard today,' he whispered.

'Where do you suppose it goes?'

'We'll find out.' Brill crouched down and stepped into the tunnel.

'Wait!' cried Segra. 'Let's arrange our capes so it looks as if we're still asleep.'

They hurried to the spot where they had been lying. They formed their capes over rocks into person-shaped bundles. Brill glanced at the window and was relieved to see that no eyes were watching. If only they could escape! He wanted to believe the tunnel led to freedom.

They slipped into the tunnel, and Segra pulled the door closed. Darkness blotted out all sense of direction.

Brill swallowed hard. 'I'll go first. Hang onto my tunic.'

'All right.' Segra's voice was laced with fright.

Brill bent his head to keep it from bumping the dirt ceiling. He stepped cautiously, feeling with his feet and hands. Some parts of the floor were stone. The sensation that he might fall into nothingness at any moment sent chills up his spine. The tunnel was narrow, and his shoulders touched both sides of the tunnel wall. He shivered as the cold and dampness penetrated his clothes.

He stopped after each step to feel the sides in case there was a door, but he only felt rough earth.

'Do you think another prisoner dug it?' asked Segra.

'I have no idea. But I wish it wasn't slanting down. I want to get to the surface.'

'I hope the guards don't wake up and realize we're gone. They'll come charging down here with their torches.'

'I wish we had a candle. Then we could go faster.'

Segra cried, 'Brill, look ahead! I see a light!'

Brill blinked. Were his eyes playing tricks on him? He thought he saw a faint glow ahead.

He moved faster. The light grew brighter as they came closer to it.

Brill whispered, 'Be careful, Segra. We don't know what we're coming to.'

A rock cave at the side of the tunnel held a candle sitting on a flat stone. Three men were lying sleeping. Shovels and a wheelbarrow stood at one side of the cave.

Brill looked down at the men's faces and felt his heart leap to his throat. One of the bearded men reminded him of his father. But it couldn't be. He was dead.

The man stirred, then suddenly jumped as he saw the children.

'Where did you come from?' he demanded, his hand on the sword in his belt.

'Who are you?' countered Brill.

The other men awakened, and they too scrambled to their feet.

The man who looked like Brill's father barked, 'We're in trouble! Our tunnel's been discovered!'

Segra explained, 'We're prisoners. We're trying to get away.'

One of the men asked, 'How did you get the door open?'

'Easy. There's an iron bar on our side. We just lifted it off,' explained Brill.

The first man groaned. 'All is lost! The minute they see these children gone, soldiers will be pouring through that door.'

Brill asked, 'What's lost?'

'Our plan to overthrow the emperor.'

'Hey, we can go back,' offered Brill. 'Nobody checks on us at night.'

'Maybe there's still hope. Hurry.' The man picked up the candle and led the way back through the tunnel. It didn't seem so long now that they had a light.

The leader asked Brill, 'What's your name?'

'Brill.'

'Brill—from the village of Grebing?'

'That's right. How did you know where I was from?'

His voice choked as he said, 'You're my son! You've grown so much I didn't recognize you.'

Brill felt a surge of joy course through his body. 'Father, I thought you were dead.'

One of the other men barked, 'Don't stop now! Our whole plan depends on getting the prisoners back before they're missed.'

Brill's father held his candle high. 'Here's the door. You go inside and bar it. In three days we'll be ready to take the castle. Listen for our signal—three knocks. Remove the bar, and our men will march in to replace the emperor with the rightful king.'

'We'll be listening,' promised Brill.

'Please don't open the door before that. Our tunnel must not be discovered before we're ready for our attack.'

'We won't,' agreed Brill.

He and Segra slipped back into their cell. Everything was quiet. They returned to lie down on the cold stone floor.

Brill whispered, 'I didn't get a chance to ask Father how he got away from the dragators.'

'I wonder if they've found King Talder's son. Your dad said they'd replace the emperor with the rightful king.'

Brill sat up. 'I'm too excited to sleep. My father's alive, and there'll be a new king. It's such great news.'

'Don't talk too loud!' warned Segra. 'I hope all the plans work out. I long to go back to the mountains to see my parents.'

'Father and I will *both* go home! Mother will be so happy to see us.'

Segra hugged her knees. 'The emperor has many soldiers. I wonder how many men are supporting the revolution. Will they have a chance?'

'They have to win. That's our only way to escape and live.'

'I'm going to sit on the bench. I wonder if I'll ever feel warm again.' She pulled her cape tight around her.

Brill sat beside her. 'It's going to be hard, just sitting here waiting.' Finally they heard the sound of boots in the corridor outside their cell. The guards were changing shifts.

They heard a soldier's deep voice. 'Good news, fellows. You'll only have one more night in this miserable hole.'

'How come.'

'Execution's been moved to tomorrow. Emperor Immane has some neighbouring king visiting him, and he wants to show him an execution.'

'I'll be glad to get out of here. I expect the emperor is proud of his unique execution method. I'd hate to have my bones crunched by a dragator's teeth.'

Brill looked at Segra. Her eyes widened in horror.

A guard placed their bowls of gruel on the sill of the hatch, but neither made a move to get them.

Brill whispered. 'Tonight, we'll escape. I'm not going to let them kill us now. I've found my father, and I want to go home with him.'

Segra shook her head. 'But if we leave, there'll be an alarm. The soldiers will find the tunnel. Your father said they'd be ready in three days. We'll ruin everything if we give them away before they're ready.'

'You're saying we should just let them throw us to the dragators?'

'I can't think of what else to do without spoiling the revolution?'

'We won't be here to open the door for them. Maybe we should try to find them tonight so that we can tell them.'

'Any time we go into that tunnel, there's a risk the guards will discover it. Can we put the bar on the hooks, so that just a little pressure from the other side will knock it off?'

He nodded. 'If we just barely rest it on the right hook, it should fall off easily. But that won't help us.'

Brill kept thinking about the dragators. He didn't want to be the last person to be fed to them before Emperor Immane was overthrown.

Segra was very quiet. Finally Brill asked, 'What are you thinking?'

'I'm praying.'

'For the executions to be postponed?'

'No, for the success of the revolution. If the emperor is replaced by a good ruler, my family can come down from the mountain. People can worship God again without fear.'

'But what good is that going to do us if we aren't here?'

'I'll be happy in heaven knowing things are better here.'

'But I don't want to go to heaven yet. Segra, we have a way to escape.'

'But if we betray the revolution before it even gets started, we'll all be executed!'

'If only we could see the future. What will happen if we let them throw us to the dragators? What will happen if we escape down the tunnel tonight?'

'We don't know, Brill. But you promised your father you wouldn't open the tunnel door.'

'I know.' Brill buried his face in his hands. He kept thinking, *There must be some way to escape without spoiling the plans to replace the emperor*. He thought until his brain felt fuzzy, but he couldn't think of a way.

That evening a guard brought them a fine meal of steak and a variety of vegetables and fruit. The soldier sat beside them on the rough bench as they nibbled at the food. Brill was not hungry; the thought that this was his last dinner on earth paralyzed his digestive system.

The guard said, 'It's a shame to see such beautiful children killed. But I can help you escape.'

Brill felt a sudden surge of hope. Perhaps this man was part of the planned revolution. 'How?'

He smiled. 'Tell me the names of the rebel leaders. They will be thrown to the dragators instead of you.'

'We didn't have anyone helping us,' answered Segra.

'Oh, come now. Two children like you could never have planned King Talder's escape. Who is the mastermind behind your treachery?'

'We don't know of any other rebels,' declared Brill.

But the guard kept questioning them.

Finally he said, 'I can't waste any more of my valuable time. But tomorrow as the dragator's teeth sink into your tender flesh, remember you could have been spared this painful death. If you tell us the names of the rebels, you won't feel your lungs filling with water as the dragator drags you to his lair.' He stood up and walked to the door. Then he turned, 'Are you ready to talk?'

'We don't know any rebels,' repeated Brill.

'The dragators are very hungry,' he said with an evil grin. He then left.

Brill began pacing up and down the cell. He had no intention of sleeping on his last night. Finally the soldiers' watchful eyes disappeared.

Now was Brill's chance to escape. But was his life important compared to the lives of all the people the emperor would execute if he remained as ruler? Brill adjusted the bar so it would fall if the door was pressed from the other side. Silently he prayed, *Dear God, I know you can help us because you can do anything. Please find a way to save us from the dragators.* He sat beside Segra.

She asked, 'You decided not to escape?'

He nodded. 'I promised my father not to open that door. I'll keep my promise, but why doesn't God answer my prayers?'

'Maybe He's planned something even better than we can imagine.'

'It doesn't look like it.' Brill's voice was bitter.

'I know. My father said death wasn't the worst thing that could happen to a person. Separation from God is worse. But no one can separate us from God.'

'I believe Jesus died for me so I'll live for ever, but I wish my stomach didn't feel so queasy.' Brill took Segra's hand. 'I'm glad you're so brave.' But he noticed that Segra's palm was sweaty, and he could hear her uneven breathing. She was scared, but she kept talking bravely to help him.

In the middle of the next morning their cell door opened. Eight soldiers escorted the children up the narrow stairs and out a back door of the castle. Bright sunlight stung Brill's eyes now used to the dungeon darkness. He breathed deeply of the flower-scented air, as the soldiers marched him towards the moat. He kept blinking his eyes trying to get them used to the brightness.

Brill saw the royal family sitting in their elaborate reviewing stand. The drummer began drumming his mono-tonous beat. Brill shuddered as he saw dragators swimming towards the bridge. He looked up at the blue sky for the last time.

The soldiers pushed the children out on the bridge. Brill reached out to squeeze Segra's hand. She looked at him and smiled a weak smile. 'It'll soon be over,' she whispered.

'God is with us,' he answered in a choked voice.

A large crowd had gathered on the other side of the moat. The emperor stood to give his customary remarks.

'I, the Exalted Emperor of Exitorn, proclaim that ALL rebels shall die—whether they be men, women, or children!'

Brill recognized Florette's plaintive cry. 'Please don't kill Segra!'

The emperor thundered, 'This girl has bewitched my daughter. Throw her to the dragators!'

Florette screamed as the soldiers lifted Segra up and dropped her over the side of the bridge. Then Brill felt strong arms grip his upper arms, lifting him up, over, and then he fell.

Before he hit the water, a dragator caught him between the pincers of his large jaws!

12

Underwater Surprise

BRILL FELT THE SHARP TEETH, but they weren't clamped together enough to cause pain. The dragator dragged him under the cold water. Down, down, down they went until Brill's lungs felt as if they would burst. Instinctively he took a breath, but water rushed in, stinging his nostrils, choking him. The blackness of unconsciousness blotted out his terror.

Later, he heard voices.

'I saw his eyes flicker. He's coming to.'

'Did you get all the water from his lungs?'

'I did my best.'

Brill opened his eyes to see two men looking at him. The rock walls of a dark cave surrounded him. One man held a candle.

'Segra!' Brill gasped. 'Where's Segra?'

The man pointed to Segra, who knelt on the four-foot ledge and patted a scaly dragator in the water. She called, 'Look, Brill—it's Peachy. He brought me here.'

Brill breathed deeply, hoping the air might help his aching head. 'Good job, Peachy,' he called.

The taller man said, 'Better wave to Chanto. He's the one who carried you. He always wants to know his charges are all right.'

Brill waved to the large dragator by Peachy. 'Thanks, Chanto.' He looked up at the tall man. 'Don't dragators eat people after all?'

'No, they *like* people—all except the emperor and the people who forced them to live in the moat.'

'Let's move inside,' suggested the shorter man.

'Where am I?' Brill asked.

'You'll hear the whole story in time. You need to get these wet clothes off. Come on.'

Segra bent and kissed Peachy's scaly head. 'I wish I had a basket of peaches for you.'

'Feel strong enough to walk?' the short man asked Brill.

'Yes.' But as Brill stood, a wave of dizziness washed over him.

The taller man grabbed his arm. Slowly, they walked through the narrow passage which ended in a small room where a rope ladder led upward.

'Can you climb the ladder?' asked the man.

'I'm OK.' The dizziness was almost gone and Brill was anxious to see what was at the top of the ladder.

He climbed behind Segra, listening to the rumble of voices above him. He looked around as his head came to the level of the floor. A crowd of people milled about in a large cavern.

His father took his hand and helped him up. 'Brill, are you all right?'

'I'm fine.' Brill stepped into the room, and his father threw his arms around him in a quick hug. 'It's so good to see you again.'

'We won't be able to open the door, but we fixed the bar so that it will fall off when you push on the door,' explained Brill.

'Thanks, Son. I'm sure we'll manage.'

'Did Grandfather get rescued too?' asked Brill hopefully.

Father put his arm around Brill's shoulder. 'I'm afraid the fall from the drawbridge was too much for some of the older people, Brill.'

Brill swallowed hard. 'You mean Grandfather...'

'His bones were brittle and many of them broke. He lived a few days, but then he slipped away to be with the Lord.'

The ache that Brill felt on the day of Grandfather's execution returned. His eyes clouded with tears, so he didn't notice King Talder until he said, 'I'm sorry about your grandfather, Brill. Before he died, he told me, "God is calling me home, but you still have work to do." He was a brave, good man.'

Brill smiled through his tears. Peachy hadn't drowned the king after all! If all went well, Talder would rule Exitorn again.

Father took Brill's hand. 'Come into my room and put on some dry clothes.'

Father led the way to a small cave off the main cavern. He handed Brill a large tunic. 'It'll be too big, but it's dry, and you can wear it while your clothes are drying by the fire.'

'You can throw out my silk tunic. I'll be glad to wear my homespuns again.'

'You will want to come home with me then?'

'Oh, yes! Father, do you have time to explain how you all got here?'

His father sat on a flat stone. 'First of all, dragators are intelligent beings. They can't speak to us, but we're amazed at the things they understand. They long to escape from the moat, and get back to the rivers where they're free. They know their best hope is to overthrow the emperor. So every time the emperor threw someone to them, they rushed him to the natural caves under Palatial Island.'

Brill sat beside his father. 'How do you get food down here?'

'There's a tunnel which leads outside the city. We have friends there who help us by sending food—enough for the dragators too.'

'It's amazing that the emperor never realized the dragators weren't eating the people he threw to them.'

'Not when you understand that Immane has no true friends. Even those with important jobs live in fear that Immane will some day have them thrown to the dragators. If they know the dragators aren't killing their victims, they don't want Immane to change his execution style.' Father stood up. 'Come, let's join the others.'

As they came to the main cavern, they joined King Talder who was talking to Segra. The king said, 'I want to thank you both for all you did for me.'

Brill smiled. 'I can hardly believe that most of the people thrown to the dragators are still alive.'

'It was still a terrible experience,' added King Talder. 'I'm very glad I didn't have to be thrown into the moat. My brittle bones might have snapped.'

'The king arrived at an important time,' said Father. 'He showed the men where to dig to reach that door to the castle.'

'When I was a child, I sometimes played in these caverns,' explained King Talder. 'But my father thought they were too dangerous, so he had the tunnel leading to the caves filled in.' The king moved on to talk to others while Brill and Segra shared their surprising experiences when they were thrown into the moat.

Later the king signalled for silence. Though his skin was wrinkled and his hair grey, his eyes glowed with determination. 'The time is close,' he said in a deep commanding tone. 'Tomorrow night, we will enter the palace, capture the royal family, and I will return to my throne. The emperor and his family will be exiled. We hope to avoid bloodshed.' The crowd cheered, and he held his arms out to them in a symbolic gesture of love. 'Freedom will be restored to the enslaved people of the empire.' He turned to Brill's father. 'What are the latest reports from the city?'

'The rebels there are ready. Most of the people will be glad to swear their allegiance to you.'

The king smiled. 'God has led us this far, and I know He will continue to lead. We have reconstructed many parts of the Holy Book from the memories of all of you, and it will again be our guide. Love for God and for one another will replace the forced allegiance to a selfish emperor who governs with fear.'

The crowd cheered.

Segra whispered to Brill, 'As soon as King Talder is back on the throne, I will go back to my parents and my mountain.'

Brill nodded. 'And I will go back to the farm.'

Segra called, 'What about the dragators who made this all possible?'

'They will all be transported back to the rivers from where they came,' promised King Talder. 'They too will be free. The moat will again be used for canoeing on warm afternoons. God's hand turns darkness into light, sorrow into joy, and hopeless circumstances into great victories. I pray that He will help me find my long-lost son, so there will be an heir to the throne.'

Brill squeezed his father's hand. 'Now that I've seen what God can do, I won't be so afraid.'

*   *   *   *   *

On the day of the revolution, the caverns filled with city people who were anxious to overthrow the emperor. Brill saw Newfel, the soldier who had brought him to Palatial Island.

Brill whispered to him, 'Are soldiers rebelling too?'

'Most of them. A few are waiting to make sure which side wins, but there's no doubt about the outcome. Not many men are still loyal to Immane.'

Father asked Brill, 'Where do the members of the royal family sleep? I have a floor plan of the castle which King Talder drew.'

Brill pointed out the royal bedrooms. He also showed where soldiers were stationed.

'You've given us valuable information,' said his father, who was organizing the men into squadrons to take various parts of the castle.

Brill was assigned to the men who were to arrest Prince Grossder and his servants.

At midnight the men began moving up the tunnel towards the palace dungeon. The bar fell off the door in the cell where Brill and Segra had been imprisoned. The door leading to the hall was not locked for the dungeon was empty.

The men streamed into the corridor and marched up the stone stairs. Brill was behind the lead soldiers, and his heart pounded as he heard a man shout, 'Throw down your arms and welcome King Talder back—Ahhh!'

A scream sent a chill through Brill. Had the soldier been killed? He could hear the crash of swords.

'Send for more soldiers. We can't hold them.'

'I'm not fighting for the emperor. Here's my sword.'

'What's happening?' Brill asked a tall man.

'Our men have overcome the guards. Come on, let's go.'

As they passed, Brill saw one of the rebels lying wounded. Another man was bandaging his arm. But the guards had surrendered their swords. One called, 'Good luck to you.'

As planned, Brill led his troop to Prince Grossder's room. He saw a few palace soldiers, but none were fighting. As he stepped into the familiar room, he called, 'Prince Grossder, wake up! You're being sent into exile!'

The prince uttered a strangled cry. 'A ghost! Help! Meopar, help me!'

But Meopar and the other servants had already been captured. The invaders were tying their wrists together.

'My father will have you all thrown to the dragators!' screamed Grossder.

The rebels paid no attention. Brill helped Grossder dress as he muttered curses and threats. The men propelled him to the throne room where Immane, Queen Lera, and Florette were assembled to meet King Talder.

Immane sputtered, 'You'll pay for this, Talder! I'll chop off your head—you and all your rebels. I have hundreds of soldiers outside who are loyal to me.'

A man stepped forward to report, 'Your soldiers killed the men who swam across the moat to lower the drawbridge. The rebels who control the city have not been able to reach Palatial Island.'

'Good, good—there's still hope!' cried Immane.

'I'm afraid not, your majesty. In the struggle with the rebels one of the chains broke, so the bridge was hanging partly in the water. The dragators crawled up on it and on to the land. Swords can't penetrate their tough hides, and they've chased your soldiers to the roof of a storage shed.'

Immane shuddered. 'Dragators loose on land? They must be pushed back to the moat. Nobody's safe with them running around.'

'Immane, you no longer rule Exitorn,' said King Talder. 'We do not fear the dragators; they saved us from your sentence of death.'

Immane pounded his fists against his forehead. 'How could I have been so fooled by the dragators? They ruined my kingdom!'

'No, Immane, your own selfishness defeated you.'

'What will happen to us?' asked the queen, dabbing her eyes with her lace handkerchief.

'You and your family will be taken to the Island of Pover,' answered Talder. 'Your servants have their choice of whether to go with you or remain here. Most of them say they prefer to stay here.'

'But how can I get along without servants?' demanded Immane.

'I expect you'll lose some of the fat you've accumulated. You'll have to work for your food. I'm sending a supply of seed and farm tools with you.'

'I'm no farmer,' said Immane in a choked voice.

'Pover has a good climate for farming,' said King Talder.

'Will cacao beans grow there?' asked Grossder

'I don't know,' answered King Talder.

'I can't live without chocolate!' cried Grossder.

'We have a lot worse problems than worrying about chocolate,' snapped Immane.

Segra put her arms around Florette. 'I wish you could come with me,' Segra said.

'I wish so too, but Mother needs me. Some day we'll meet again.'

'You'll always be my friend,' whispered Segra.

'I'm so glad you didn't die,' Florette said and smiled. 'At least I won't have to marry Prince Oplack.'

Father put his arm around Brill's shoulders. 'Come, Son, let's go home. I've borrowed a cart.'

Brill asked, 'Father, can Segra come with us? After we've seen Mother, we must help her find her family.'

'Of course, Brill. We won't forget all that Segra's done.'

Brill felt a surge of excitement. 'I can't wait to get home. Mother will be so surprised and happy to see us.'

Life in Exitorn

Belay: To secure a rope by winding it around a tree or other object.

Cacao beans: The seed of the cacao tree used in making cocoa and chocolate.

Canopy: A rooflike covering, such as the spreading branchy layer of a forest.

Dragators: Imaginary animals who live in rivers like alligators but have long necks and legs like dragons.

Exile: A prolonged living away from one's country often as a punishment.

Goose quill pens: Pens made from sharpened, stiff goose feathers. They are dipped in ink for writing. The quill is the hollow horny stem of a feather.

Gruel: Thin broth made by cooking ground grain, such as oatmeal, in water or milk.

Gutteral sound: A harsh sound formed in the throat.

Horn inkwells: Containers for ink made from animal horns.

Interrogators: People who ask questions. The term usually applies to police, soldiers, or others acting in their official capacities.

Ire: Anger.

Manoeuvres: Planned movements of troops.

Monarchs: Rulers of kingdoms or empires.

Mother-of-pearl: The hard, glossy lining of the shell of the pearl oyster and certain other shells. It is used to make buttons and other ornaments.

Peasants: Poor farmers.

Predecessor: A person holding an office or position before another.

Produce: Something which is produced, especially fresh fruits and vegetables.

Purge: To rid a nation of people held to be disloyal or undesirable.

Scribe: A penman who copies manuscripts. Before printing was invented, many scribes were needed.

Tool: To impress letters or designs on leather with special tools. Books or other items with such designs are said to be tooled.

Treachery: Betrayal of trust or allegiance. Disloyalty.

Tunic: A blouse-like garment extending to the hips or lower, usually gathered at the waist with a belt.